Heart in Your Hands
Emma Humfleet

Author's Note

This novel contains profanity, graphic sexual descriptions, and sensitive topics including miscarriage. This book is intended for readers eighteen and older.

There are all kinds of love in this world but never the same love twice.
— F. Scott Fitzgerald

Table of Contents

Chapter 1
Tatum

"No," Asher said, loud enough to turn the heads of everyone in Frothies. "I am a firm believer that marriage and kids have a habit of ruining lives and relationships. I'm never going down that shitty road."

I knew he felt my dagger stare through my dark sunglasses as he sipped on his sickly sweet iced vanilla latte with extra whipped cream and caramel drizzle. At 18, Ash liked his coffee exactly how an eight-year-old likes their dessert, drenched in sugar and sweetness–his guilty pleasure that he took no shame indulging in every time we went to Frothies, the most "hip" place in our small Michigan town, Cardinal Springs.

This had become a weekly routine for us after school. I'd work on my homework while he'd ogle me from across the table, cracking jokes trying to distract me. It worked more than it should have, but I liked having him with me. His presence made me feel content even when we weren't saying anything.

Asher and I had been friends since elementary school. He meant more to me than anyone on this planet, which is probably why it felt like a knife digging into my chest listening to him ramble on about how marriage and kids would, "never be a part of my future, Tate."

Maybe that's part of the reason why he and I didn't find ourselves romantically involved until the previous summer. We always had that friendship where we tested the limits of our platonic boundaries without actually doing anything further: stolen looks here, a feather light touch there. He did almost kiss me once during a game of spin the bottle, but he found an excuse to get out of it and kiss Mallory Thomas instead.

We both knew we had a thing for each other back in freshman year, but we never wanted to take that next step and risk screwing it all up. Now here we were at the edge of adulthood on opposite sides of two of the most important things in my life: marriage and children.

It shouldn't have come as a surprise. I was quite literally the most opposite of Asher that a human could be. We couldn't have been more different if we tried, but everything came so naturally for us. I'm a short blonde with curves, brown eyes, and some meat on my bones. I wouldn't call myself fat, but I'm definitely not a dainty thing. I wasn't the prettiest girl around, but I like to think I was above average. I wanted to go to college and get my bachelor's, hell, maybe even a master's degree if I had the means. I wanted to get married in a pretty white dress while my dad walked me down the aisle and build a family with a baby or two. I hardly ever cussed unless you consider "hell" a curse word. I'd gotten straight A's all through school, and I liked my coffee bitter and sugarless–which is how I sometimes come across to people from what I've been told. Except to Asher. He always told me I was misunderstood, because he understood me when nobody else did.

Asher was everything I was not: tall with piercing green eyes, curly dark hair, and ridiculously attractive. He was six foot three with a strong muscular build. Don't get me started on his arms. The sight of them alone made me want to climb him like a tree. Skipping a day at the gym was nearly torture for him. He turned the head of basically every girl he passed. Granted, that's not a ton considering our town was all of five hundred people, and everyone knew everyone. That's part of the reason why I wanted to go to college so much. I wanted to get away from the small town gossip and the "What is he doing with *her*?" whispers.

College did not exist in his future. In fact, he would have probably bragged about his 2.0 GPA if you asked him about it. He wasn't dumb; he just didn't try. His sister Ari, pretty much my only other friend, was the one who got good grades and did whatever extracurriculars she could that would look good on a college application. Sometimes I think I wore off on her instead of Asher with my "live up to your potential" speeches. She had the bubbly outgoing personality and lived in the spotlight.

Asher had no problem letting her while he stayed back in the shadows. Other than the gym, there wasn't much that Asher was passionate about, except for photography. Putting a camera in his hands was like handing Picasso a paintbrush. It was a talent that lived in his blood. Though to him, he didn't see the beauty of his work like I did. One of his favorite subjects to photograph was me, and while I didn't have the highest confidence, his photos made me feel beautiful, like I could finally see what he saw when he looked at me so adoringly with those panty-dropping eyes.

He had never travelled much as a kid despite the fact that his family had the money to go anywhere they wanted to. Other than their home, his parents didn't live a lavish lifestyle. They were modest with their money. Apart from the times when he'd go with me and my brother to visit my mom in Florida, Michigan was the extent of his travels. He wanted to change that though. He wanted to see the world and what it had to offer, feeling like he had missed out during his childhood. Countless times I urged him to use photography as his way to do it, but he always brushed me off saying his work wasn't good enough, and it would never amount to anything.

If you'd have asked each of us what careers we wanted, my answer would have been journalist or a novelist, while his would've been, "Uh, I don't know. Whatever I can get, probably." He never saw how much potential he had no matter how hard I tried to show him.

So how did this candy flavored coffee drinker and I come to be in a romantic relationship? We just gave in to what we knew was inevitable. I think we both needed to know if it would work, and we couldn't continue without ever knowing. We danced around the idea without vocalizing it for several years. Neither of us really dated anyone else. Asher had the occasional hookup, but from what I gathered, it was never more than casual sex for him. I got that he had needs, but that never dulled the ache of finding out that someone else had been in his bed instead of me.

I had never even had sex until Asher. He was my first everything. My first kiss, first date, first hookup. I know several people thought I was lame for being a seventeen year old virgin, but Asher didn't. I think it always felt wrong thinking about doing any of that with someone who wasn't him. He was my safe place, my sanctuary. He knew everything about me just like I knew everything about him, even the parts I didn't like and chose to ignore.

A part of us both knew we were fated to fail from the beginning, that we wanted different things in life, but something kept us from acknowledging what we both knew. We loved each other too much to see the wrecking ball before it hit. There was love and there was attraction. So much attraction. He knew what he was doing in the bedroom, that's for sure. He was man candy if I'd ever seen it, and he definitely looked like candy underneath me. I could have devoured him every day if given the chance. Blame it on teenage hormones.

He took his time learning what I liked, learning every part of my body, especially the ones that made me feel insecure, and paid extra attention to them. He tried his best to rid me of my insecurities which only made me love him more. Made me want to marry him and have his children even more. Exactly the opposite of what he wanted.

"Tate!" he snapped. "Are you even listening to me?"

No.

"Yes."

"Seriously, Tate. Do you really enjoy the idea of being legally tied to someone for the rest of your life? You can't do what you want when you want without worrying about someone else."

His stupid question was dragging me out of my daydream. Suddenly I was fuming with anger at his insinuation that he couldn't do what he wanted to do without worrying about how I fit into the equation.

"Let me ask you this then," I said. "How would being married to me be any different than what we are now? Am I holding you back?"

He looked at me with a hint of confusion. "I mean, I wouldn't say you hold me back, but—"

"But what?" I snapped. "There is no 'but' here. Either I do or I don't. Apparently being married is too much to ask because you have to consider someone else, and how they fit into your decisions. Either you want to be with only me or you don't."

I could feel his anger level rising as I watched his jaw tense.

"That's not the only difference, Tate, and you fucking know it. You're twisting my words into something I don't mean. We would be legally bound to each other. We couldn't just walk away if it went south. Divorce is expensive and fucking stupid. I want to travel. I want to see everything there is to see. You can't do that with a kid."

"So you think we would end up divorced."

"What the fuck? No," he about yelled. "Will you just stop? You're turning this into something it's not."

9

He took a long sip of his no longer iced latte.

I couldn't help the downward spiral that I felt coming. This conversation was making me see my life, my future with him, looking through his lens. Even though I had always known he didn't want the same things in life, I guess I was always being naive about it, letting my love for him cloud my vision thinking one day he would want me the way I want him. Legally. And forever. I didn't like what I saw when I thought about how he pictured the future, our future. I suddenly saw myself being thirty-five, ending up divorced to the man I thought loved me as much as I loved him. I saw myself without any kids, by myself with nobody but me to take care of.

"No, Asher. I won't stop. Why are we even together?"

He was shifting in his seat, clearly uncomfortable with where this conversation was going, especially since our "discussion" had gotten the attention of pretty much everyone in the place.

"Can we maybe talk about this somewhere else?" he asked, nodding in the direction of our audience.

Asher leading the way, we silently walked to Finley Park to the overgrown garden where we had first kissed. He took my hands in his and took a deep breath.

"Tate, I love you. I do. But, what the hell is happening here? You've known for years that marriage wasn't in my future. Now you're giving me an ultimatum that if I don't agree to marry you and have kids, we're done? That's a lot of fucking pressure, Tate. We're eighteen for god's sake. I don't know what I'm doing with my life after graduation, let alone a five year plan. I'm not like you."

I could have just agreed with him, kissed him under the statue of Admiral Finley, and enjoyed the last few months we had until I left for college. But I didn't.

"Why don't you want what your parents have?" I pressed. "They have the perfect marriage, the perfect family, the perfect life, the perfect kids. I don't want all of that tomorrow, but I'm a planner, Asher. I want you to be part of my plan."

I wanted him to say, "Yes, Tate. I'll marry you, and I'll put babies in you and you'll write and I'll take photographs and we'll travel with our perfect family and…" but that's not what he said.

Instead, he said nothing.

I could feel the tears starting to form in my eyes. I looked away to keep him from seeing the pain in my face. I knew what was about to happen. Frankly, I think I always knew it would end like this, but we both needed to see that for ourselves. So I said the worst thing I could: "Have I been anything more than an easy fuck for you the past year?"

That got him talking again.

"Did you seriously just ask me that?" he spat. "You know I fucking love you, but I'm not going to change my entire being into what you want me to be to fit into *your* agenda. So you be fucking honest here, Tate. It sounds like you don't want to be with me, and if that's the case then fucking say it."

That had me snapping my eyes back to him as the tears started to escape down my cheeks.

Instead of saying, "You are my safe space! You are who I wanted to be beside me every day until I die," I said, "I will never be enough for you. I will always keep you from what you want in life, and you will always keep me from what I want."

Admiral Finley looked out across the park ignoring the apocalypse at his feet.

"We talk about something that we've talked about a million times in the past four years," he said, "and suddenly you're ending our whole relationship based on a fucking ultimatum? Everything we have had is as good as gone to you. Nice, Tate."

"We don't want the same things," I said to my own feet. "We knew this was a bad idea from the start, but we let our feelings cloud our judgement."

The tears were still welling in my eyes, blurring my vision. Things weren't blurred enough to keep me from seeing Mr. Sugar and Sweetness walk away from Ms. Bitter and Sugarless without saying another word. I couldn't stop my heart from hurting or my eyes from burning. Even though I knew it was the right thing, it felt like I was dying.

✛

It had been hours since we broke up, and I still couldn't stop crying. Suddenly it was like I couldn't picture my future at all if it meant not having Asher in my life. He was all I had known for six years. I needed him. Even if I had to give up everything I had thought I wanted, I didn't want a life without him. Maybe I didn't need to get married or have kids to feel fulfilled. I would still go to college, get my degree(s), and be successful. So what if he didn't want to get married. We would still be together.

Kids. I was 18-years-old and arguing with my boyfriend–ex-boyfriend?–about kids. I had to fix this, but I didn't want to go running back to him like a helpless girl who can't survive without her boyfriend. I decided to give it a week. If I still felt like I was dying without him, I would talk to him.

I felt pathetic thinking about the fact that he'd survive without me. He was popular and no shortage of girls like Shauna Gates or Mallory Thomas who would jump at the chance to be with him. He was always having fun going out to parties with the football quarterback douchebag Johnathan Beck. Of course I never went because they were on school nights.

He had his photography, a talent so strong I envied him for it because I don't have a creative bone in my body. Envisioning my future without him, I saw nothing. His sister was my only other friend, and losing Asher meant losing Ari in a sense, too. He had a life without me in it, but I couldn't say the same. I didn't have friends, I didn't have hobbies or clubs. He was my life jacket, and without him I felt like I'd drown.

✝

That week was a bit of a blur, but I spent a lot more time with my dad and 12-year-old brother Jace. I helped Jace with his 7th-grade English homework, tried to help my dad on his always-breaking-down truck, read way too much about activities and clubs on campus, and even tried to write–although they were all teen romance stories.

Asher called me a few days into my Asher-free week, but somehow I managed to fight every urge in my body telling me to answer and beg him to take me back. Dad kept asking me what was wrong, but I couldn't talk to him. My dad loved Asher like another son.

My emotions were reeling, and I needed to talk to someone who wasn't my dad or kid brother, or, God, Asher's little sister.

Tears fell down my cheeks as soon as she answered.

"Hi, honey."

"Hi, Mom," I said through a choked breath as I held back a sob.

"Oh, sweetheart, what's going on?"

"Asher and I broke up."

I immediately regretted calling her because I knew she didn't like Asher, but I needed to vent, and saying it out loud had me clutching my stomach as tears continued to roll down my face.

I expected her to say something about how Asher doesn't have a future anyway and how he's all brawn and no brains, but she didn't. A moment of silence passed before she spoke up: "I'm sorry honey. What happened?"

I offered her the explanation, reliving the argument all over again in my head as I told her everything.

"I miss him so much, Mom," I blubbered. "It hurts so bad, and I don't want to feel like this anymore."

"Oh, sweetheart. I hate hearing you talk like this. I know you're hurting, but it will get better. When your father…" She stopped herself. She knew I hated it when she talked about Dad. "You just have to give it some time. You don't want to be with someone who can't give you what you want."

Mom and dad have been divorced since I was eight. She claims now the reason is because they weren't compatible anymore, but I'd learned the truth of it all is she cheated with some guy she went to school with. My dad to this day won't speak an ill word about my mom, but I know she resents him. Dad couldn't give her what she wanted, and she ran almost 1,500 miles away to escape. I was only eight and Jace was three. I was still trying to forgive her for that.

My brother and I spent half of our summers and our spring breaks with mom in Florida and the rest of our time was with dad back in Michigan. Mom wanted to move to Florida to the warmer weather, claiming that was where she needed to be after the divorce, so they came up with a custody agreement to stay out of court.

"You're young," she continued. "You still have time to figure out who your soul mate is. You'll come here for college and you'll meet a new guy who will sweep you off your feet and give you the future you've always dreamed of. You just have to let it happen."

I knew she only meant well, but her words felt like a knife to the gut. Let it happen? I didn't want to wait for another guy. I wanted *my* guy.

I thanked her and she told me she loved me.

✛

I tried to hear what she had said, but after a week had passed–yes, I made it a whole week– I ignored my mom's advice and I picked up my phone.

Those six words coming from the voice I had missed so much brought tears to my eyes.

"Tatum, come back to me, baby."

Twenty minutes later I was falling into his passenger seat. He drove us in silence until we got to our spot. It was this cute little area tucked away in some trees next to the creek that runs through town.

As soon as he had the car in park, I was on him. I couldn't hold back my tears as I climbed across the armrest of his truck to straddle his lap. We didn't need to talk. I just needed to touch him, needed to feel him. We needed each other and nothing else as we apologized to each other without words. I was fumbling with his zipper as he was pulling down my sundress, peppering needy kisses across my chest before pulling my taught nipple into his mouth, making me arch back accidentally hitting the steering wheel and pressing the horn. We should have looked to see if anyone was around, see if we had drawn attention to ourselves, but we didn't care. Lifting up on my knees, I shimmied my panties down my legs, breaking our kiss just long enough for him to tear his shirt over his head. He pushed his jeans down his thighs allowing his cock to bob free. I took him in my hand, pumping from base to tip, moaning when a drop of pre-cum gathers. I wiped it off with my thumb and brought it to my mouth savoring the taste of him on my tongue. Fire burned in his eyes as he gripped my hips in his hands and lifted me up aligning himself with my entrance.

I was already slick with need, desperate to feel him inside of me, to feel whole again as he pieced me back together. He did exactly that as he grabbed my neck pulling my mouth to his, capturing my lips in a feral kiss as I lowered myself onto his throbbing dick. His fingers dug deep into my hips as if he was afraid that if he let go I'd disappear. I laced my fingers through his curls, gripping his hair and pulling so that his eyes met mine as I bounced on his cock. I saw the forgiveness in his eyes as he stared back at me. I could see that I was still his. Releasing his hold on my hips he reached up, kneading my breasts in his palms. I lowered my hand to rub my clit while gripping his shoulder to keep my balance. Seconds later he stilled inside me as he spilled his release. I rubbed my clit harder, allowing my climax to take over. Placing his sweat slicked forehead to mine, he whispered "I love you." before pulling my sundress back up, gently putting the straps back in place. We were going to be okay.

When he drove me home a few hours later, we could feel our connection more than we ever had. Our lives were bound together no matter what either of us thought. We were meant for each other. Famous last words.

☦

The next three weeks flew by in a blur as I stressed about finals and started organizing things for my move to school in the fall. Graduation was in a week. Asher and I had been doing great since that night in his truck. It was as if our argument hadn't affected us at all. Not in a negative way anyway. He had decided he was going to wait a year and work full time before he started traveling so we could focus on ourselves as a couple while I was in school. Then I could travel with him over the summer and visit wherever he was on my breaks. It was going to work.

I was sitting at the kitchen table prepping for my last final when I couldn't get my feet to carry me to the bathroom fast enough. I had barely gotten the lid of the toilet lifted before I was emptying the contents of my stomach. I hurled until there was nothing left.

I never got sick. It didn't make sense. I had been getting a lot of headaches and an upset stomach the past week or so, but I figured it was because of all the stress from studying. It wasn't until I saw the box of tampons next to the toilet that I started to panic. My period was late. No, it couldn't be late. I was always on time. It had come at the same time every month since I was thirteen.

An hour later I was staring at six pregnancy tests, each with two blazing pink lines. After the first five, I finally admitted that they probably weren't false positives. I was pregnant. My heart was fighting a battle as I thought about what this meant. Asher would freak. But I couldn't deny as I looked at my stomach in the mirror, I was excited to see myself grow this little life. I knew Ash didn't want kids, but now that he didn't have a choice, would he change his mind?

I didn't know how he would take the news, especially after our argument a few weeks ago. We had been doing so well, I didn't want to ruin it, but he needed to know.

I was on his doorstep an hour later trying to control my shaking knees and my urge to vomit. Whether that was from nerves or the child growing in my womb I didn't know. I was about to burst into tears when the door started to open and I realized it wasn't Asher, it was his mother.

"Are you okay honey?" she asked, taking my hand. "You don't look good."

The look in her eyes almost had me running back to my car, but I knew I had to tell Asher.

"Yeah, I'm fine, Mrs. Clemson. I'm just stressed from finals. Is Ash around?"

"How many times have we been over this, dear? Call me Elizabeth."

"He just left a little bit ago. I think he said he was going to the gym. Do you want to wait inside until he gets back? Ari is in the kitchen if you want to visit with her for a bit. I just made some brownies, too."

The thought of consuming something so sugary made my mouth water and my stomach churn at the same time. I'd be lying if I said I hadn't thought about running away from his doorstep and never stepping foot near it again, but I knew if I did that I'd never forgive myself.

"That would be nice," I said, stepping inside. "Thank you."

Making my way to the kitchen, Ari's smiling face had my stomach in knots. Even though she's three years younger than me, she and I had become quite close over the years. Like I said, other than Asher she was pretty much the only friend I had. The desire to talk to her about my problem was strong, but I couldn't ask her to keep a secret of that magnitude.

"Hey!" Ari said as she shoved a piece of brownie in her mouth.

"Hey. What are you working on?" I asked as I surveyed the papers strewn across the kitchen island.

"Geometry. Please explain why I need to prove why a triangle is a triangle. Because it's a freaking triangle, that's why!"

"Still not a fan of math, huh?"

"No. But I have to be good at it if I want to stay on the honor roll. If I don't get an A on this final, I'll drop to an A minus. I'll break my perfect record, and I'm not letting a freaking triangle be the reason."

"Grades aren't everything, honey," her mom said as she busied herself tidying their outrageous kitchen. "You know we'd still be proud of you with an A minus."

"Yeah, well being proud doesn't get me into college, Mom." I hid my chuckle because I saw so much of myself in her.

What would I tell Ari if she wanted to marry her boyfriend? What would I tell Ari if she got herself knocked up during make-up sex?

"Hey, do you think when I'm done you can drive us to see a movie or something?" she asked me. "I need a mental break."

My heart sank because I would much rather take her to see a movie than think about the bomb I was about to drop on her brother.

"I'm sorry, Ari. I can't today. I have to talk… have to finish prepping for my last final."

Her face dropped and the fact that I was letting her down killed me.

"What am I going to do when you go off to college? You're the only person keeping me sane. You better come visit all the time. Or better yet, I'll come to Florida to visit you. We can have beach days!"

"I would love that," I cooed. And I meant it, but I knew beach days would look nothing like she was imagining.

Seeming content with my answer and my forced smile, she went back to her studying as she shoved another piece of brownie in her mouth.

"So... how are things with you two?" his mom asked. "He's seemed really happy lately. I wasn't sure if that was entirely because of you, or if the new job had anything to do with it."

The mention of a new job had me stopping in my tracks. Ash hadn't mentioned anything about a new job. I took the opportunity to pry.

"He just hasn't gotten to tell me what it's for, or where exactly he will be going," I said, shoving a brownie into my mouth.

"Oh. The new start up magazine," she said as if to jog my memory. "They haven't made it big yet so they can't pay him a fortune or anything, but his travel is paid for. I guess it's more of an internship. I think for the most part he will just be in different parts of Southern California for now, but they plan on sending him out of the country within the first year if everything goes to plan. My cousin lives in San Diego, so Asher won't have to worry about paying for a place which he really wouldn't be able to do on the salary they're giving him."

"Oh," I managed to say. "Right." A job. Literally across the country. What the hell? There was no way I was leaving that house until he got back.

✝

I sat in his room preparing myself for the argument I knew was coming and waited for him to get back. Almost two hours had gone by before he was walking in covered in sweat from his daily gym ritual.

"Hey babe," he said as he walked up to me, pressing a soft kiss on the top of my head. He must have taken my silence as a sign that something was wrong.

"You okay? Mom said you seemed off when you got here."

He took off his shirt tossing it on the bed, and his sweat-covered muscles had me losing focus. Pregnancy hormones are no joke.

"Yeah, you know I'm actually far from it," I said, shooting my gaze to the floor to look at anything but his figure.

"What's going on? Did you forget about a final or something?"

His slight chuckle had me wanting to throw punches. He clearly had no idea that I knew he was keeping a huge secret from me.

"No," I said. "Actually, I'm just thinking about how my *boyfriend* decided to hide the fact that he's taking a job across the country from me right after he agreed to take time for us."

His face paled slightly, but he recovered quickly. "Mom told you?" he said. "God, that woman can't keep her fucking mouth shut about anything."

"Yes, she told me! She thought I knew!" At this point, the pregnancy was the last thing on my mind, and I couldn't keep the anger from spewing. "So was all that crap about taking a year off and working on us some big facade? You wanted me to think this was all going to work out when in reality you had a completely different plan all along?"

I started pacing, a technique my mom told me to use when I was overwhelmed. "You get in my pants and then tell me we're going to be this amazing power couple, but really you were just planning on leaving me behind."

The pacing wasn't working.

"What?" he blubbered. "No. I didn't know about the internship when we made that decision. I forgot I had even applied for the position. It was months ago. I didn't even tell you when I applied because I knew it was a long shot. I wasn't even going to apply, but you're the one always telling me I don't push myself, utilize my full potential."

He was right. I said things like that to him all the time, and now here he was following my advice and breaking my heart simultaneously.

"I hadn't heard anything after a couple of months so I just assumed I didn't get it and moved on," he continued. "Then a few days ago I got an email asking me to do a virtual interview. They lined it up for the next day and offered me the position almost immediately afterwards. I sent them my portfolio, and I guess they were really impressed. You've been studying, so I haven't had the time to tell you yet."

"I don't think moving across the country is something that you wait to tell someone," I shouted, worried now that his mom or Ari might hear me. "Especially your girlfriend!" I whisper-yelled. "I mean God Ash, do you even think about anyone but yourself?"

"I thought you'd be happy for me, not pissed the fuck off," he said, sitting down on his bed, defeated. "I thought you'd be glad I was doing something productive with my life."

"This isn't just about you anymore!" I said, reflexively holding my belly.

"What the hell is that supposed to mean?"

I should have told him then and there and just gotten it out, but I couldn't get myself to tell him anymore. I knew it would destroy him. Ash didn't want kids, but he also was not one to walk away from responsibility as big as this was. Essays, finals, picking Ari up from softball. Those were responsibilities he would ignore. This was not. He would've hated me for getting pregnant, but he'd have stayed just because he felt like he had to. He wouldn't have been happy. It would have ruined any chance of him ever doing what he wanted in his life. There was no point in bringing it up anymore. I would figure it out on my own.

"Nothing," I said instead. "I just mean that you made this huge decision about what you were going to do with your life, and you didn't even have the decency to tell me. You only thought about you. Typical."

And with that, the brownie was ready to come back up.

When I returned from the bathroom, Ash wasn't in his room anymore. I went downstairs to find him sitting with Ari in front of a plate of brownie crumbs.

"I was just telling Ari that you were considering a gap year before going to college so you can travel with me," he said.

I couldn't believe what I was hearing. College had been my dream for years, and he expected me to give it up and move to California? That was not the plan.

"But then I said that might not work," I said, picking at a brownie crumb. "Remember?"

"But you *agreed* I'm not the only one who has to give something up for us to work," he said through gritted teeth.

"Is this a private conversation?" asked Ari.

"No," I snapped. "You should hear this. You should hear how your big brother is not the one who busted his ass for six years trying to keep a 4.0 GPA. That he's not the one who gave up most of his free time to study and do extra credit!"

"Are you serious right now, Tate?" Ash asked.

I tasted a twinge of crimson as I realized I was biting my bottom lip too hard from my frustration, but I wasn't finished.

"Serious about how you haven't gotten higher than a C on any assignment? Serious about partying and drinking on the weekends, not giving a shit how it looks?"

"She has a point, Ash," said Ari. "You–"

"Shut up," he growled. The look in his eyes was something I had never seen before. It was a mix of anger, hurt, confusion, and desire. Yes, he was mad, but he was turned on too.

"On that note, I'll see myself out," she replied. "You two enjoy."

Ari out of the room, Ash stood up and came over to me. I could feel his hot breath on my face as he was getting mere inches from me. He kept getting closer until my back was against the kitchen wall. His eyes were dark with anger and desire.

I knew he wanted me, and I'd be lying to myself if I said I didn't want him too. I wanted to feel his lips on mine, and feel his hands trail up my body. His head came down and he nipped at the skin on my neck. I could feel my heart rate picking up as his kisses climbed up my neck and he began nibbling on my ear. His breath and body was hot. I could smell the sweat on his skin from his workout. It was making it hard to focus on why I was here and where this conversation had been going. His lips were hovering over mine. His tongue swept out to wet his lower lip and my brain came back to reality. I needed to end this before I ended up upstairs in his bed again. Or worse, confessing everything to him, and ruining everything.

"This isn't going to work," I said, as I pushed my way around him and back to the open space of the room. I had to force myself to say, "We had a fun year, but that's all it was. It was fun. You're going to take the job, and you're going to forget that we ever had this *thing.*"

I knew that was the only way he was actually going to hear what I was saying. I didn't want to give him the chance to say anything else. I knew if I stayed, I wouldn't be able to hide my confession anymore. I'd melt into his arms all over again.

I ran out of the house to my car, my cheeks still streaked with tears.

That was how it had to be.

Chapter 2
Tatum
8 years later

⋅◆⋅

"Oh Tatum," my mother beams. "That's beautiful! That's it; that's the one."

I try to refrain from giving a snide remark at her comment. That exact phrase has left my mom's mouth six times. Every dress I've tried on has been *the one.* Of course, every dress I have tried on so far has been one she picked out. I'm staring at myself in the mirror mortified, feeling like a damn cupcake covered in glittery buttercream frosting. Not to mention the horrifically itchy tulle underneath has me wanting to claw my skin off.

"Could you at least try to like something you try on?" she pleads. My mom doesn't even try to hide the irritation in her voice at the fact that I've hated every dress she's loved on me.

"It's just not my style, Mom," I say in the large ballgown with a six foot train, glitter tulle overlay, lace flowers covering the bodice, and of course a matching belt so bedazzled it would blind everyone the second I walked in the sun. "They're all too..." I search for the word. "Frilly for me. You know I don't like frilly. Or glittery, or poofy." And this one is all three. Staring at my reflection in the mirror, it looks like I'm drowning in tulle rather than being accentuated by it.

"Why don't we try your pick, Tatum?" the consultant asks.

I can see the sympathy on this poor woman's face. Relief floods me as I realize I can peel myself out of this horrific gown my mom is pushing me to fall in love with, and into the one that I know will make me happy.

"Fine," she gives in. "Let's see what you picked then."

The contempt in her tone only makes me want to try on *my* dress more. I only picked out one dress compared to my mother's seventeen. She had shown up before I had, just to make sure she had plenty of time to pick everything she wanted me to try on. Which to my mother was practically everything in the damn store that has a gigantic price tag and is entirely too heavy.

My mom has always had this vision in her head of what my wedding would look like. I'm pretty sure she started planning my wedding before I even turned seven. In her mind, I was going to walk down the aisle of an enormous cathedral in an overly poofy ballgown with a fifty foot train and long veil hanging over my face while a flower girl dropped fresh petals beneath my feet.

I get it. My mom never got a big fancy wedding when she married my dad. They didn't have money, and my grandparents couldn't offer much help, so they ended up with a backyard ceremony as my mom recited her vows in a dress from JC Penney. I think she's secretly always resented my dad for it, and why she's living vicariously through me with my wedding.

She has planned out every detail. All the way from the venue down to the flower centerpieces for each table. I'm pretty sure she had already written out the guest list and had it hidden in her stash of wedding plans somewhere before I was even engaged.

Alone in the dressing room, I admire myself in the mirror, running my palms up and down the fabric, fingering the low hanging neckline, checking out the even lower back. It clings to my body in all of the right places to show off my curves without making me feel fat unlike the cupcake gowns that make me feel like a weeble wobble toy.

It also has a gorgeous slit that goes mid thigh. It's everything my mother hates, and the thought has me curling in my lips trying to hide my grin at the fact that I'm finally controlling something about this wedding. I'm comfortable in my skin, which is something I hadn't been for a long time. I feel sexy in the dress, and I don't want to feel any other way.

I fight to conceal my grin as I walk out. I know my mother is going to hate it. I, however, couldn't love it more.

"Absolutely not, Tate." she announces. "You cannot wear that."

"Why not?" I say, spinning in front of the mirrors. "It is *my* wedding after all, and I happen to love it."

"It does look beautiful," says the consultant. "*And* it's on sale."

"You cannot seriously like that sale dress more than the last one," she says.

"Actually, I do," I say bravely. "It's simple and much more my style."

"You looked so beautiful in that last dress though, like a princess," she pleads. "Don't you want to feel like a princess on your special day? It isn't even white."

She's right. It's not white. There is no glitter, no long train, no uncomfortable tulle, and it is much more revealing than she would ever approve of.

"Who says I can't feel like a princess in this dress?"

"I don't think any of the Disney princesses had white dresses," says the consultant. Score.

Still, my mom persists. "Do you really want to wear *that* for your wedding? The one and only wedding you'll get and you want to wear that? You're getting married, not going clubbing. Besides, I don't think Cayson would approve of you walking down the aisle in that."

Without even looking back at my mom, I turn to the consultant.

"I'll take it."

I hand over my debit card to pay for the gown with a smile on my face. She's right, Cayson will probably hate it. It's not classy enough for his taste, but I don't know why he'd have any complaints because I look fucking incredible in it. He should be drooling over me when he sees me walking down the aisle in my dress. I don't think he'd disapprove of it nearly as much if my mother hadn't already drilled her ideas into his head.

Carrying the dress bag to the car, my mom won't stop talking about how bad of a decision I've made getting that dress.

"I told you I'd pay for the dress, Tate. If money was the problem I would've covered it. You didn't have to get a two hundred dollar hoochie coochie dress."

Hoochie coochie? The condescension that lack of money is the reason I chose a gown I loved pisses me off, but I also know that she wishes she would've had the offer she's giving me when she was in my shoes. Shoes. I could offer to let her buy me shoes.

I stay quiet though because she will keep arguing if I talk back. I love my mom, but after the *incident*, our relationship never went back to normal. She became more judgmental and critical of everything I did. She's built this idea in her head of what everything in my life should look like, and I let her.

It started small by buying me clothes that she approved of, ones she said suited me. Even though they weren't my style, and honestly I hated most of them, I wore them because it made her happy. Then she started bringing me meals she cooked for me, claiming she had extra and she knew I was too swamped to cook for myself, but I know she wasn't cooking extra of the flavorless tofu garbage she typically brought over.

When she signed us both up for a gym membership insisting we work out together, that's when I really started to feel the judgement in her ways, her persistence to shape me into what she wanted. At one point I found out she had made a profile on a dating app for me and lined up dates with multiple guys claiming she did it because she could tell I was lonely. I started to draw a line there, refusing to go on the dates with the bankers or realtors or, gag, personal trainers she'd found for me. There was Tad who invested in crypto and Gunner who had been the personal trainer for Melania Trump, and Price, the lawyer who said he was "into chubby chicks just to piss off my mom." She even went to the extent of sending in job applications on my behalf because she said my retail job wasn't utilizing my full potential. She doesn't think my current job does either, but she also thinks I'm a virtual assistant, not an intimacy advice columnist.

Things were rough for a while, but we were getting better once Cayson came into the picture–maybe she had run out of things about me she wanted to change–but the wedding planning seems to have put a huge kink in our improvement. She wants me to be happy, but she only wants me to be happy on her terms.

I should be happy. I am happy. My fiancé Cayson is the perfect guy on paper. His parents basically raised him in a country club, and I'm sure he will be due a hefty chunk of change when they pass, but he does well for himself even without their money. He takes care of himself, he dresses like a catalog model, gets two hundred dollar haircuts, and even treats himself to manicures. He's got that handsome businessman attractiveness going for him. He's a little on the shorter side standing at about five foot eleven, though he will tell you "six foot on a good day." He plays golf and tennis.

While Cayson comes from wealth, has a great work ethic, and wants a large wedding and family. Cayson is exactly who my mom would have picked for me if she could have hand picked him herself. In fact, I swore I recognized him from somewhere when I saw him in class and had convinced myself that he was one of the matches from the dating app that my mom was trying to pair me with. That's why it took him three times of asking me out to get me to agree. He fit into my mom's vision perfectly and it felt too crazy that he would've fallen into my path naturally without her manipulation.

We have the picture perfect relationship. We both have great jobs, bringing in a decent income to support ourselves. Of course, he brings in more than I do because I'm only working part time while I finish up my MFA.

Cayson and I both have the same goals on our timelines, syncing perfectly. College: Check. Start our careers: Check. Get engaged: Check. Get married. Have a few kids.

"Are you even listening to me?" My mom is staring at me like she hasn't been droning on about pointless shit for the last ten minutes as we walked to our cars.

"Yes, Mom, I was listening," I say. I wasn't. "Can we just go grab some lunch please? I'm starving."

"Let's get açaí bowls from that new smoothie place."

"I don't want a smoothie for lunch, Mom. I want carbs."

"Don't think I haven't noticed that you've put on a few pounds. You're going to regret not getting a dress with a corset if you keep that up."

I grit my teeth and huff but keep my mouth shut as I lay my dress across the back seats and drop into the driver's seat.

"I'll meet you there," I lie as she climbs into her obnoxiously large SUV with a smug grin on her face as if she's won.

I stop at Taco Bell before heading home instead, curling up with my latest romance novel on my Kindle. I also happily ignore her texts once she realizes I've stood her up.

My actions may seem childish, but she's always had a bad habit of picking on my weight ever since my pregnancy. Like somehow being eight weeks pregnant had made me gain enough weight to noticeably change my appearance. Of course it didn't, but it doesn't seem to bother her when she's hurting my feelings now. I wouldn't have even told her about the baby if she hadn't been there when I started bleeding. I'm not stupid enough to think I could have hidden my pregnancy from her forever. But I definitely hadn't planned on cluing her in until I had figured everything out. I didn't want to upset her, but from the way her behavior towards me has changed since the loss, it's obvious that didn't work in my favor.

I started bleeding during one of my visits with her, and I couldn't control the panic in my voice as I told her I needed to get to the hospital. She drove me there in complete silence and never once offered a comforting word. At least she loved me enough not to break me with her harsh words. At least at the time anyway. Sometimes it feels like she won't love me the same if I don't live my life exactly the way she wants, which sometimes makes me regret moving so close to her.

I loved Florida though. I knew from the first time I visited that it was where I wanted to be, so I moved there for college after high school but took a gap semester after I lost the baby. My mom was livid about that decision, and she made sure I knew about it. My dad still thinks it was because I didn't know what I wanted to do with my life, that I couldn't pick a concentration. That isn't entirely a lie. He apparently has never heard of having an undeclared major.

My mom let him believe that was the case because she didn't want anyone to know about the baby, and I mean nobody. She happily accepted that Asher was no longer a part of my life, and having his baby would've prevented that. She probably would have tried to convince me to put the baby up for adoption. Anything to keep Asher out of the picture. She loved that I was states away from him. She told me we weren't right for each other, and there was someone better waiting for me to find him.

And I did. I found Cayson. Steady, secure, reliable Cayson.

Chapter 3
Asher

"Yeah, Mom," I groan into the phone. "I will try to be there, but I'm not making any promises."

My sister's engagement party is this weekend, and my mom seems to think it will be a catastrophic disaster if I'm not in attendance.

"Well, you haven't been home to visit in months and if you can't even be here for Thanksgiving dinner then the least you can do is be here for your sister's party."

I know there's no point in arguing with her so I repeat myself before hanging up: "Like I said Mom, I will *try* to be there, but no promises."

Ari and I are close, but I'm pretty sure she'll survive if I'm not there. She knows I don't like coming home, and she knows why. Though if you asked her, she'd say it was my fault. It was hard enough to get my mom to buy my excuse for why I couldn't come home for the holiday. Not that I don't want to see my parents and Ari, but sitting at a table listening to them dote on their perfect daughter who is doing everything right and is happy as can be just sounds repulsive.

I'm glad she's happy, but it will inevitably lead to my mom's questioning about if I'm seeing anyone and pressing me about my job at the firm which is an interrogation I don't want to deal with. So as far as my mom is concerned, I'm staying back in California so my boss can help me study for the Bar exam, not sitting in my apartment watching Netflix and eating Ramen.

I don't know why my parents are throwing her a party anyway. She's only twenty-three, so I don't understand why she's getting married. Ari has always been the marriage type though. That's probably why her and my ex got along so well. But hey, if she wants to commit to fucking one person for the rest of her life and being tied down by a legally binding piece of paper then so be it. If she wants to be like our parents, miserably married and living like roommates, the more power to her.

I am decidedly NOT the marriage type. There's only one girl I ever saw a potential future with and she broke my heart eight years ago. I've been content being a single man ever since. I still enjoy sex, but that's all it ever is.

I tried the "coupling" thing once with a girl a couple years back, and it didn't end well. We hooked up a few times before she started calling me the B word. I had to put a stop to that real quick. She was good in the sack but she wasn't *that* good. Plus I'd be lying if I said I wasn't picturing *her* the entire time we were fucking. The only reason I was even drawn to her in the first place was because she reminded me of Tate with her blonde hair and curves. She was smart, too. Most guys would have said she was a package deal: tits and a brain. But I couldn't get myself to see a relationship with her. It didn't feel right; granted, nothing has ever felt right since Tate.

Tate is the only girl I've ever loved. We were best friends since the fifth grade. Well, I guess it would have depended on who you asked. She would say she hated me the entire first year she knew me, but that's a lie. We had assigned seats and she was lucky enough to be in the desk in front of me. I thought she smelled nice and I wanted to be friends with her so I irritated the fuck out of her every chance I got.

I used to stick stuff in her thick blonde ponytail and let her go the whole day until someone would ruin it and tell her. I stuck gum in her hair once and she threatened to stab me with the scissors she used to cut it out.

She was always so anal about her pencils being sharpened so I would steal them from her desk and replace them with ones that had broken lead. I think that stupid prank alone pissed her off more than anything else I did.

I knew that girl was special when I told her she looked nice one day and she told me to "Kiss my butt." Insulting, I know. I think it hurt her ten times more to say the words than it did for me to hear them. She hardly ever cussed, even to the last day I saw her. She thought her comment would get me off her back, but really it just made me fall for her. She would never admit it, but she had fallen for me too. She was everything I wasn't. Everything I should have wanted to be: persistent, smart, driven. God, she was beautiful, too.

We became inseparable that year. She and I would hang out every day after school at her dad Charlie's house and then at Frothies, this coffee shop that pretended it was some fancy french cafe. Miss goody two shoes wouldn't talk to me until she finished her homework though. All while she nagged me to do mine. When she was home, we'd hang out all day. We'd walk down by the creek or we'd ride down the country roads in the bed of Charlie's truck when he got home from work. We spent almost every day together from sixth grade until high school graduation. There were even a few times I went with her to visit her mom, Mia, in Florida. Then we get serious and Mia decided I was trash.

We had danced around the idea of getting together for years. We both knew we had feelings for each other that were more than platonic. We would have killed for each other if we had to. We just clicked. She was my whole world, though I'm not sure she realized it at times. Plus we were always finding reasons to be close to one another. I'd brush her hand and pretend it was an accident, or she'd "squeeze" past me in a space that was definitely *not* tight in her jeans that definitely *were* tight. I'd be lying if I said there weren't a couple of times that she caught me with a hard on from looking at her ass or her tits. I can't deny her curves got me going. Granted, everything about her got me going.

The summer before senior year I got the nerve to kiss her. We were sitting in my truck at our spot by the lake tucked back by some trees and I just did it. She had been rambling on about something I wasn't even listening to–I know, real gentleman, huh– and I couldn't stop staring at her lips as she talked. She was wearing the perfume she knew I loved. She smelled like jasmine and vanilla, and she was wearing a pair of jeans that hugged her hips beautifully. I couldn't stop thinking about my mouth on hers, wanting to know what she tasted like. And she always did this thing where she bit her lip when she was frustrated. God, that was such a turn on for me, and she kept doing it during the story she was telling me.

She looked at me to see if I was listening and I just lunged at her, planting my lips on hers. At first she pushed me away and asked what I was doing, but I just smiled and kissed her again. She resisted it at first before she realized what was happening and then she melted into me deepening the kiss. We didn't have sex that night, but we did get rather handsy. Any other girl would have gotten in my pants, but Tate wasn't just any other girl.

If I'm being honest, I knew I shouldn't have made the move to turn our friendship into something romantic. I knew Tate wanted to get married and have a big family after she went to college. I didn't want anything along those lines. I knew it was a bad idea to take things further with her, but I couldn't help how much I wanted her, how much I ached for her. I loved her more than I thought was possible, and I couldn't handle the idea of letting her be with someone else.

The next day she made me have the conversation about what that meant for us and what would happen to our friendship if we broke up. I hadn't known if we were going to work. In fact, there were several reasons I knew we probably wouldn't, but I didn't care at the time and hoped that if we didn't work, I wouldn't lose her completely. It didn't work out that way.

Honestly, if you'd have asked me about marriage my senior year, I would have said that I could see myself marrying her one day down the road, but she didn't know that. I probably would have married her eventually to make her happy. But I know how she is, or was. Even if that meant having a five year engagement while she went to college, she would have wanted a rock on her finger immediately if she had any inkling that I was even *thinking* about the possibility of marriage.

Tate was a girl full of adventure and desire. She knew what she wanted, and she'd set fire to the world to get it. She set goals for her life, even ones ten years down the road, and she set her sights on achieving them. She even told me that she would be the salutatorian when she graduated. Not valedictorian; salutatorian. Something about how people who come in second place make the best leaders.

Even with small things, she had this ability to decide in the moment when she wanted something and she wasn't afraid to go for it. One summer we were out walking one of the country roads when Tate found this little kitten meowing in the field. I watched her eyes as she made the split decision to gather the tiny ball of fur in her arms and carry it with her as if nothing had even happened. As if that cat had already been a permanent fixture in her life. I couldn't help but laugh when she named him Mushroom, petting behind his ears as he clawed at her hands. She's allergic to cats, but even as she broke out in hives, she looked at me, and looked at that cat like her world was complete. Tate just wanted to be happy and I admired her for that, but hated that it was also the straw that broke the camel's back and tore us apart.

Tate idolized my parents' marriage. From the outside looking in I can understand why she did. They seemed like the ideal couple with a beautiful life: great careers, a nice house, two kids. Tate knew almost everything about my life, but that is one secret I kept to myself. My parents were anything but perfect. Frankly, I've never understood why they have stayed together, especially now that their kids are older and out of the house. It's like they love seeing the other one miserable.

They thought we were naive enough to believe that they were happy, but I wasn't stupid. I heard their arguments when they thought we were in bed. I saw Mom pour shots of vodka in her water bottle. I watched Dad sneak out of the house late at night more times than I could count. We never took family vacations because they couldn't stand each other long enough to take a trip with each other. Tate always saw my mom in the kitchen greeting Dad with a kiss on the cheek as he came home from work smelling like his assistant's perfume. She saw my dad opening the car door for my mom when we went to the mall for back to school clothes. They played their parts well because Tate fell for it all, and I let her. Tate saw the picture of happiness that she had wanted from her own parents.

Crushing her vision of love would have caused more damage than I was willing to cause. She always wanted to get a degree, get married and settle down with kids, just like the happy couple who couldn't stand one another, Elizabeth and Mark Clemson.

Tate had watched her parents go through a rough divorce when she was just a kid, and I think that was what made her want a family even more.

She wanted to show her kids what a healthy marriage looked like and succeed at something that her parents never did.

I don't know that I will ever regret telling her I didn't want children. Having kids would have held me back from pursuing the career I wanted. I didn't see kids in my future when I imagined it. Plus, I didn't want to share Tate with anyone else. She was mine. A child would've ruined all of it.

When she brought the topic up again a few weeks before graduation, I didn't think it was that serious. We were both freshly eighteen with so much life to live, so much to experience. Apparently I was wrong, and it was very serious because somehow a normal conversation about our future turned into a breakup. She was so pissed that I didn't want to get married or have kids as if she hadn't known that about me all along.

Like I said, I knew it had been a bad idea to get involved with her. I let her go because being honest with myself meant admitting that she was better with someone who would give her everything she wanted, everything she deserved. I wanted her to have the world on a silver platter, but I couldn't give it to her. So I gave her space. But, I've never been very good at being honest with myself so I tried calling her a few days later hell bent on getting her to see it my way. Stubborn woman that she was, she didn't answer me.

A few days later I was sitting in my truck talking myself out of turning the key and driving to her house to make us a thing again. Not in a manipulative "I'll kill you if I can't have you" sort of way, but I didn't want her to be with anyone else. Before I had the chance to convince myself to park my truck and get her back, my phone lit up with her name. I picked up, not letting her say a word before I told her to come back to me. I drove around the neighborhood for another fifteen minutes so she didn't realize I had actually already driven most of the way to her house before she called.

That was one of the best nights and the best sex I'd ever had, but now that memory is colored by the reminder of her. The reminder of the affect she had on me, and the way my body and heart reacted to her every time she was around. The way it felt like she was the breath in my lungs that kept me going. The stabilizing force in my life that kept me grounded.

I drove her home that night and she told me she couldn't have a family if that meant not having one with me. She didn't want anyone else. My possessive mind loved hearing those words which just proves how fucking stupid I was for thinking that she'd given up entirely on her ultimatum, that she'd give up everything she wanted for me.

Things were pretty good for the next couple of weeks that followed. We decided that she could go to school in Florida and I would take a year before traveling so that we could work on our relationship. I would work and save up money, and then after her freshman year she was going to come visit me on my travels during her breaks.

Tate was so busy cramming for finals that we didn't end up talking about our fight any more. When she wasn't studying, I was burying myself in her.

A week before graduation she showed up at my house while I was at the gym. If my mom hadn't been there to open the door, things may have never ended the way they did.

My mom has a big mouth so I'm not surprised she spilled the details of my internship to Tate. Granted, I probably should have told her before I told my mom, but things were going so good with us that I didn't want to ruin it.

I had gotten an offer from a company, Pure, that was working on a startup magazine called Global Hipster, and they wanted someone to take photographs for the covers. My photography teacher had recommended me. I guess his sister's husband's brother was best friends with the owner of the magazine, and when he found out they were looking for an intern, he suggested I apply. I had sent in my portfolio to Pure months before and never heard anything so I just assumed they had picked someone else. I was proud of my work, but I wasn't a professional by any means; mostly photos of places Tate and I loved in Cardinal Springs. Okay, mostly photos of Tate. Still, I saw my photography as a meaningless hobby that would get me nowhere in life. Tate always swore I was wasting my potential, that I had so much talent behind a camera.

If it wasn't for her constantly being up my ass about trying to make a career out of it, I wouldn't have even applied, so I was completely shocked when I got the email about setting up an interview.

The day she found out about the job I had never seen her so pissed off. I tried telling her that she was being irrational–great idea, I know. She could have taken time before starting college and gone with me. She kept telling me that I didn't understand and that I was being selfish. There was no talking sense into that woman. She left in tears and I let her.

If anyone was being selfish, it was her. I had finally done something to live up to her hopes for me, and even still it wasn't enough for her. I loved her, but I hated her for walking out on me like that. A huge part of me wanted to grab her ass and haul her back to my bed until she forgot she was mad at me. I may have been lazy and bad in school, but one thing that I wasn't was selfish. I'm still not. I'm a giver just as much as a receiver in more ways than one if you catch my drift.

We didn't see each other after that fight. I didn't go to graduation even though I knew I'd see her if I went. I had no desire to see her after she left me standing in my room like an idiot. If she wanted to forget everything we were, so be it.

I lost track of her after I moved to San Diego that summer. She had never been one for social media which made it hard to keep tabs on her, especially since I've never been huge on socials either. I can't count the amount of times I picked up my phone with my finger hovering over the call button on her name. I eventually had to delete her number so I'd stop being tempted. I cursed myself a million times for that in the first two years.

My life-changing internship didn't pan out. After a year, not only was I not making enough money to survive, Global Hipster was a flop; I knew it wasn't practical to expect that photography was going to be a stable income so I changed paths. Of course Tate didn't know that because she didn't have enough faith in me to stay and find out.

I kept hope for a while that I would run into her in our hometown on one of my visits back home. Cardinal Springs is so small that I would have known if she came back, and my sister would've been the first to let me know. Ari has always blamed me for losing Tate as a friend. Tate didn't just disappear on *me* the day she walked out, but Ari is too nice to hate her for it.

Tate never came back to that small little town that she used to call home, where she used to love me. I could have asked Charlie where she was and I don't doubt he would've told me. We had always gotten along really well. I've always wondered how he took our breakup, but I felt too awkward afterwards to keep in contact with him.

I could have reached out to Mia to see where Tate ended up, but that bitch never liked me so she probably would have lied to me anyway. She never did anything malicious to me, but she made it clear I wasn't what she wanted for her daughter in a long term sense which is ironic considering I swear she hit on me the last time I went with Tate to visit her on spring break our senior year.

Call me crazy, but she dropped several innuendos, giggled at my jokes, and talked far too much about the flexibility she had as a cheerleader that she still has to this day apparently. There were also several subtle touches throughout the visit that seemed too coincidental. Tate didn't pick up on it and I never told her because if anything is a relationship killer, telling your girlfriend you think her mom has a thing for you will definitely kill the vibe, and if I'm being honest, her mom always gave me cougar vibes. Eventually that hope of seeing Tate again faded and I was just left with the anger of her leaving and the way she doubted me.

I

New Message

To thirstwithclarissa@gmail.com

Help

Dear Clarissa,
My girlfriend and I have been dating for nine years. We are high school sweethearts and are both 24 years old now. She's upset we aren't engaged yet and told me she's going to leave me if I don't propose in the next six months. I don't feel like we are ready for marriage yet, especially financially. I love her and don't want to lose her, but I also don't want to base our future on an ultimatum. What should I do?

Chapter 4
Tatum

◆◆◆

"Come on honey," my dad pleads. "I haven't seen you since I came to visit you in Florida two years ago."

My dad has been pestering me to come home for a visit ever since I admitted I needed a break from wedding planning.

"You haven't been home in eight years, Tate. You hardly ever see your brother, who misses you by the way. I miss my daughter, and you've been going MIA on me a lot lately. I know you could use the break. Plus you work from home so it's not like you can't bring your work with you."

"We see each other all the time, Dad," I explain even though I know I'm about to be talked into something I don't want to do.

"Besides, Jace couldn't care less about seeing me, and you'll see me in a few weeks for the wedding. You already said you'd come down a day early."

Luckily this isn't one of our usual Facetime calls so he can't see me rolling my eyes because I know where this conversation is going.

"Facetime doesn't count, and you know it. I want to spend time with my daughter. Jace does care about seeing you despite what you think. You're still his sister, and he loves you."

He knows that's a lie considering he complains every week about the distance that college has put between him and Jace.

"Dad, Jace only cares about sucking face with a new girl every week."

"Well, even he agreed to come home for the weekend, so why can't you put in the same effort? You know there aren't going to be many more

45

opportunities that all three of us will be able to coordinate time off to be together."

Shit. He knows how to make me feel guilty when he needs to. Asshole.

"Besides, I want to see you before the wedding," he goes on. "We both know that you will be so busy getting things ready that we won't be able to spend time together before the big day. And frankly I'd rather be able to see you without Cayden hovering the entire time."

My dad has only met Cayson in person once, but he sees him almost every time we video chat, and I know exactly what he means about the hovering, especially lately.

"It's Cayson, Dad, and Jace lives an hour away from home. That's not exactly the same as getting on a plane and flying home." I sigh as I sink onto the couch.

"I'll pay for the ticket," he says. "If you don't want to use vacation days, visit for the long weekend coming up for Thanksgiving. Just tell me you'll at least think about it. You can't stay away forever."

His comment has me burying a groan because we both know what he's trying to say. I'm not staying away. At least that's what I keep trying to tell myself every time my dad tries to convince me to come home for a visit. A coward would hide away from their home town out of fear of seeing their ex boyfriend who they haven't seen in eight years. I am not a coward. Am I?

Dad doesn't know about the baby, but he connected the dots that Asher had to be the reason I have refused to come home for the past eight years. He just assumes I'm scared of running into Asher one day. He's not entirely wrong, but I'm not going to fill him in on the details. Besides, I'm engaged now. It's not like I still have feelings for someone I was with so many years ago. I am happily engaged to the love of my life so the past doesn't matter. As far as I know, Asher still lives in California and is probably dating–but obviously not married to–some tanned model, and I wouldn't run into him back home anyway.

"Sure, Dad. It's a long weekend coming up with the holiday so I'll think about it."

"Thank you, honey. I'll talk to you soon. I love you."

"Love you too, Dad."

It'll only be for the weekend, I tell myself though I know convincing Cayson to let me off the hook for Thanksgiving is going to be a challenge. Thanksgiving is his family's favorite holiday. Every year they help host a Thanksgiving dinner at the country club, and every year I've been I have hated every minute of it. Can't miss that.

I haul my ass off the couch to finish my work for the day, eager to share my Clarissa Rivers intimacy advice so I can spend my evening in my oversized tee binge eating the ice cream in my freezer.

Chapter 5
Tatum

My mom hasn't left me alone about finalizing wedding details since we went dress shopping a few weeks ago. She wants everything to be fairytale perfect. You would think it was her wedding with how obsessive she's become about the whole damn thing. Hell, I would've been content going to the courthouse at this point. I've never needed a big fancy wedding. I used to think about it a lot in high school, but my mom's obsession with my life has made it all a bit lackluster to me now.

However, since my mother has offered to pay for it and take the reins, my motto has been, "sit back and let her." Well, with most things, even down to having a December wedding, which is pointless in Florida. Not my gown though. I never intended on letting her get her way with the dress. The woman about went into cardiac arrest when I went against her will and bought the two hundred dollar gown straight off the clearance rack. It's the one thing she hasn't gotten her way on with this wedding, and the fact that she's still fuming about it makes me giddier than it should.

It's been two weeks since my dad begged me to come visit for the holiday weekend. I texted him this morning and told him he could book a flight for Thursday. I'm surprised he even managed to get a ticket for the holiday, but I decided there's no reason for me not to go. My column isn't due until Tuesday so I'll have enough time to work on it while I visit, or on the flight home. Besides, even if Asher somehow made his way back to Cardinal Springs, I don't plan on leaving my dad's house anyway.

"Why do you have to go *this* weekend?" Cayson asks, scrolling through our registry online. "You'll miss Thanksgiving dinner at the club! Just wait a few months until I have time off to take with you."

The mention of the holiday dinner makes me cringe. My dad never made a big deal about the holiday growing up, so being surrounded by snobby rich families who want to be catered to on the holiday isn't really my thing.

Cayson also isn't thrilled about the idea of me going back to Michigan alone. He's been dropping hints for a while that he wants to see my hometown and see where I grew up, although he has this idea that everyone is a farmer and there's no internet. He has no idea why I've been so adamant about staying away.

"It needs to be this weekend," I tell him. "Jace will have finals in a few months and dad has a lot coming up with work so he's going to be busy."

I can see he's frustrated but he's trying to contain it.

It's not that I don't want to take him with me; I just need some space to myself. The wedding plans have been suffocating me lately, and I'm struggling to keep up the excitement that he needs and deserves from me. A weekend to myself to decompress should help with that.

He's not the argumentative type which I've learned to appreciate. If we do argue, he's always the first to apologize.

"But the wedding is in three weeks," he continues. Maybe he is the arguing type. "There's still so much that needs to get done. If I went with you, we could work on it together."

"Babe, my mom has everything under control with this wedding. I'm sure she'd be more than happy to hash out the details with you. She just loves you. I just need a weekend, okay? Between work and school and everything else I just feel like I'm drowning and I need to find my breath."

Walking over I take his face in my hands planting a small kiss on his lips.

"I promise when I get back, we will talk about everything you planned out," I say. "You've been doing a great job with it all so far so I trust your decisions. Besides, you know the dinner at the club makes me anxious. It's so prestigious, and all of those people make me antsy. I'll even come back and make us a special dinner just for us."

I take his hand in mine and plant another soft kiss on his lips. That seems to be the reassurance he needs because he doesn't fight me on it anymore. Instead he grabs my suitcase from the closet.

"Let me help you pack at least."

Wednesday night has rolled around and I'm making sure I have everything packed for my flight tomorrow when my phone rings. Almost instantly I regret answering.

"He's your fiancé, Tate," my mom chides. "There is no reason for you to be going alone. Just wait a few months after the honeymoon and go together. Your dad will survive. Plus, you know how important the club dinner is! We always go together and it will be weird if you don't go."

I know the reason my mom really doesn't want me missing the dinner is because it's another opportunity for her to parade me around, shoving my obnoxiously large engagement ring in people's faces and bragging about the upcoming wedding. When I look at Cayson, he gives me a face of guilt, likely because he talked to my mom about the fact I wouldn't postpone my trip. I guess he wasn't as okay with my decision as I thought.

"Mom," I say as motherly as I can, "it's my decision and I miss dad. I haven't seen him in ages. Cayson will survive, too." I take a second to give him a "won't you?" look. "I already told him I guarantee you'll be more than happy to finalize the last minute details with him and I'll come back eagerly waiting to hear all about it. You can take him to that açaí place you love. Plus, you're still more than welcome to go to the dinner. You know you still have an invitation."

I hear her huff on the other end of the phone and I know that I've won this argument. Giving her full rights to plan whatever she wants while I'm gone is music to her ears.

"I'll see you when I get home," I say. "Love you."

I press end call and toss my phone on the table as I make my way over to Cayson who is now pouting, clearly upset I haven't changed my mind to stay home with him instead.

"It's not a big deal, babe. It's three days. I'll be back Sunday night and we can spend the evening together before we start the work week."

"It is a big deal," he whines. "We get married in three weeks, and I want to spend time with you."

His constant need for attention is really starting to get on my nerves. It's like I'm engaged to a fucking golden retriever. His desire to be around me used to be endearing, but lately it has turned suffocating.

"Besides, I was hoping we could maybe... you know? Have some fun this weekend."

He throws me a wink and I suppress a chuckle. Cayson is the man I'm going to spend my life with which is why my ring finger is weighed down with a two carat diamond that my mom helped him pick out. But one thing for certain is I am not marrying him for the sex. His version of "having fun" is doing it missionary in the dark with zero talking. No dirty talk, no switching up positions. In fact I think if I asked him to choke me or pull my hair, he'd keel over. It's just his three minutes of grunts until he's done, followed by a, "I love you so much" and then he's ready for bed. That happens about once a month.

Not to mention the man has no knowledge or desire for foreplay. The one time I tried to get him to go down on me, he said I wouldn't need it because he knew what he was doing and I would be "totally prepared" as he kissed me for all of thirty seconds before shoving it in. Only one of us got an orgasm. My vibrator spends more time in my pants in a week than my soon to be husband has in our entire relationship.

At first, I thought it was going to be a deal breaker. But then I realized as long as I have a couple colorful toys in my nightstand, I'll be fine. Most men wouldn't know where *it* is anyway even if I had gotten with someone else. Every hookup I had after high school was always a dud and ended with me finishing myself off at home. They were all pigs who just wanted a quick fuck without giving a shit if I finished. Honestly, only one guy has ever been able to get me off. The first and only guy to ever give me an orgasm. If I needed a man to give me an orgasm to survive, I'd be dead by now.

That's one reason I ended up with the job I have now. If you would have asked me what I wanted to be when I grew up, a sex advice columnist would not have been the answer that came to mind. I was interning for this online magazine, Fem, senior year of college; no, the irony of that is not lost on me. Anyway, I was interning for this magazine doing mindless intern stuff, the typical fetching coffee, getting the mail, sending emails, just housekeeping really. I always sat in on their meetings to take notes, and one day my boss asked for new ideas, something to give the magazine a facelift. Don't ask me why the idea came to me, maybe a lack of spice in my own bed, but I suggested a sex advice column.

My boss loved my pitch and let me run with it. My column, Thirst, was so successful in the first year that she let me make the position remote and has promised me a managing editor position once I earn my master's. I may be shy in my own life, but putting words to paper behind a screen feels like my superpower. If I'm not having the sex life of my dreams, at least I can give other people advice on how to get it.

II

To thirstwithclarissa@gmail.com

Vibrators

Dear Clarissa,

I'm 21 years old and have yet to have an orgasm. I've tried masturbating a few times with no success. I want to try a vibrator but I have never owned one and I don't know what kind to get. I'm scared to go into a sex shop and buy one. I didn't realize how many varieties there are. What do you recommend for a newbie?

Chapter 6
Tatum

I turn my phone on and am instantly flooded with messages from Cayson that came in during my flight: *Have you boarded yet? I miss you. Let me know when you land. Call me when you get to your dad's house. I love açai bowls.* Not to mention the three voicemails that he left talking about the wedding plans he and my mom have finalized in the six hours that I have been gone.

Aren't the men supposed to hate all the wedding planning? He doesn't seem like he can get enough of it.

He has always been pretty laid back and easy to please, but ever since he and my mom have been wedding planning, it's like he is in constant need of my attention. It's not that I don't like spending time with him, I just feel like this wedding is taking away from the enjoyment of being together all the time. People take time to themselves before they get married. Right?

I can't help but break a smile when I see my dad waiting for me at the gate. He hasn't changed much since the last time I saw him in person, but it still feels strange to see the few pounds he's put on and his hair that has a bit more salt than pepper to it. Facetime really doesn't do justice for him. Sometimes I wonder why he hasn't tried dating again, but I never push the topic because I know Mom really hurt him and I don't think he ever moved past it.

"Hi, Dad."

He wraps me in a tight hug and I realize how much I truly have missed him.

"Hey, honey."

"Remind me to never fly on a holiday again. That was brutal."

I linger in his embrace smelling the scent of oil stuck to his old flannel, bringing back memories of when he'd try teaching me the ins and outs of cars while I pretended to listen and understand everything he said. I loved those hours with him growing up because I know how much they meant to him too, but I can confidently say I still have no idea how to change a tire or check my oil.

"Are you hungry?" he asks. " We can pick something up on the way home. It's early enough Sicily's should still be open."

"I'm starving," I say, my stomach audibly growling at the mention of food. "Where's Jace?"

"He's back at the house. He was on the phone with some girl when I left to come get you. We'll grab a Thanksgiving pizza on the way back. Go ahead and put your stuff in the truck and I'll order. I'm guessing pickles and mushrooms are still your favorite?"

I give him a big grin even though he looks disgusted as he remembers my go-to pizza toppings.

"Sometimes I don't know how you're my child."

He chuckles and makes the call while I climb into the truck.

I guess I should call Cayson quickly just to let him know I landed. My finger hesitates slightly over his name before clicking the call button.

"Hey!" he says after one ring. "How was your flight?"

I can hear the clinking of dishes and the white noise of the Colonial Country Club Thanksgiving soiree in the background.

"It was fine. Nothing exciting. I slept pretty much the whole flight."

"You okay? You sound off."

"I'm fine. I'm just tired from the flight. My dad just picked me up so we're gonna go grab a bite to eat. I just wanted to let you know I got here okay."

"Well, I'm glad you made it safely. I'll call you later to check in. You were right by the way. Your mom has been a huge help already. She's amazing. We'll have everything done by the time you get back."

Not that I'm surprised my mother has stepped in to finish planning, but I feel relief at the thought that he seems to be over the fact I came on this trip alone.

"I love you. I'll call you later okay?"

"Love you too. Talk later."

Silence lingers on the line before it goes dead and I hang up.

Dad climbs in the driver's seat and turns the key. The radio kicks on full volume blaring an old country song. I don't hesitate to start singing every word. I'm not ashamed to admit that country music is my favorite.

Cayson doesn't like it. I used to play it every time we got in the car, but he'd always complain about it so I only listen to it when I'm by myself. Dad joins in singing along with me and I smile as I look out the window noting how different everything is here than it is in Florida. Despite the chilly air that I've come to despise and all the leafless trees, a very small piece of me misses this being my home.

The drive to the house is peaceful as dad and I sing along to every song that comes on the radio until we stop to grab our pizzas before heading to the house.

"Jace is excited to see you," he says.

I cant help but snort because I know he's full of shit. I love my brother, but that boy cares about nothing but his next lay and what he's going to eat for dinner now that he's felt a touch of freedom. Not that dad was ever strict, but college has definitely caused him to spread his wings, and hopefully nothing else.

"You know he's going to be more excited about the pizza than about seeing me."

He laughs because he knows I'm right.

Jace comes walking out the front door bounding down the steps as I climb out of the truck holding the pizza boxes.

"Oh sweet, pizza for Thanksgiving," he says as if I'm just a statue holding the boxes. "I'm hungry as fuck. Did you get cheesy bread too? I'd kill for some damn cheesy bread."

"Jace, language."

Dad shoots him a warning look and I snort as if all three of us don't cuss like sailors now. Even at our age, he likes to pretend to play father figure and lecture us about cussing. Not because he actually cares, but he likes to act like he does.

"Are you even going to acknowledge your sister?" I ask, handing him the pizza.

"Oh, yeah. Hey, Sis. I'll take those."

He grabs the pizza boxes and heads straight back for the house, grabbing a slice from one of the boxes and shoving it in his mouth.

Before the front door is even latched I hear him call out, "Damn it! You didn't get cheesy bread! Why the fuck are there pickles on this pizza? You may as well have gotten turkey and dressing on it."

I laugh to myself and dad grabs my bag from the back of the truck.

"I told you he'd care more about the food."

Dad shakes his head and ushers me inside. Mushroom comes charging at me the second I'm through the door, rubbing his head on my leg.

"At least someone is excited to see me." I say, bending down to scratch behind his ears as he purrs.

"You're lucky I haven't gotten rid of that damn cat. He's an asshole," Dad says as he puts my bags in the hallway.

"Mushroom is not an asshole!"

"Really? Because every time I try to pet him he hisses at me. I even tried to bribe him with chicken scraps last week and the fucker bit me."

I snort at his words as I stand in front of him holding the most docile cat I've ever met. He wasn't nice to me when I first found him but we became quick buddies even though he makes me itch all over every time I hold him.

"Hmm. Must just be you. He doesn't like your bad juju."

The next few hours fly by as I catch up with Dad and Jace. I talk to Dad often, but it just isn't the same as sitting here with him. If I'm being honest, the simplicity of our Thanksgiving is much better than the holiday I would've had back in Florida.

As if his ears are burning from my thoughts, my phone pings with a message from Cayson. It's a picture of him sitting next to my mom at a table with his parents, all of them dressed to the nines enjoying their preppy party.

"Damn, did Mom get herself a new boy toy?" Jace asks looking over my shoulder at the photo. Jace and Cayson haven't met, so of course he doesn't recognize him in the picture. I hear Dad clear his throat, discomfort clear on his face at the thought of Mom having a new boyfriend.

"No, that's Cayson, you idiot. They're having dinner at his parent's club. He just wanted to show me how it's going. Mom went with him since I came here for the holiday."

Jace shrugs as he says, "Just saying, they seem awfully dolled up. They'd make a nice looking couple. Hey, maybe they're on a date."

I punch him in the arm and laugh when he audibly grunts. Looking at the photo again I don't think it looks strange. They look like they're having a good time and I'm glad he's content without me being present at the party this year. I shoot him a quick text saying, *You look nice. Glad you're having fun,* before shoving the phone back in my pocket.

"How's school, Jace? Which girl are you with now? Are you still seeing that Kara girl, or is it someone new? Oh, let me guess! There's three different ones, it just depends on the night and which class you need tutoring in. Does fucking your tutor automatically gain you extra credit?"

Dad chokes on his beer at the mention of his teenage son's sex life. Jace shoves me off the couch, laughing when I land with a thud on my ass.

"Hey! I was just joking. Kind of."

"For the record, I don't fuck any tutors," he says defensively, before adding, "Sorority girls are a different story though."

The grin on his face assures me he's not mad at me, and I love that we can still banter back and forth like this even when we don't see each other very often.

"How is school going though? Do you need help in any of your classes? There's no shame in getting a tutor you know."

"Never said there was," he mumbles. "Just don't need one." He shrugs.

"Come on, Jace. What are we talking? C average?"

"You should give your brother more credit. While I don't agree with his extracurricular activities, he's handling his own in school. You must have offered more influence on him than you think. He made the dean's list last semester."

I'm pretty sure I just audibly gasped as I turn to Jace with a smug grin on his face.

"Not as stupid as you thought, huh? Fuckboys can be smart, too. I think with my dick a lot, but I've got a brain up here too. I just pick and choose when to use it."

I throw my arms around him in a hug as he fakes a gag and pushes me away.

"My little brother is a dweeb just like I was. I never knew I was such a role model," I say walking to the kitchen to grab a pop.

He throws me a middle finger, tongue stuck out like a child as I make my way back to the couch.

Jace brought up the topic of Mom a couple more times as the night went on, but for Dad's sake I tried keeping that to a minimum. Despite the fact that he says he's moved on, I think he still loves her. He used to always say she was it for him, the one and only. She broke his heart when she cheated, but I think he still feels for her in a way she doesn't deserve.

Before their divorce, they were the picture perfect couple, at least to my seven-year-old eyes. As I grew up, I dreamed of having that type of marriage, that type of connection. The way he looked at her like she was the only woman he saw. The way they danced in the living room while Mom laughed as Dad stepped on her toes. But she wasn't happy like she pretended to be.

Dad tried to talk to me about my job, but I kept that conversation short. He doesn't need to know the details of what Clarissa Rivers does at *Fem*. I trust my dad more than anyone, but he doesn't need to know that my job involves men and women asking for advice in their bedroom, or the fact that I'm the one giving them the advice they want. I don't think my dad wants to know that last week I told a thirty-seven year old woman to try masturbating in front of her husband. Every column I write is different and some of them are rather PG-13 depending on the person who wrote in for advice, but there are several that are not family friendly, especially not for my family.

The evening continues on with a few rounds of kicking Jace's ass in Uno. We're both pretty competitive and he's a sore loser so it makes my victories much more enjoyable. Dad isn't a night owl in the slightest so he went to bed about ten o' clock while Jace and I stay up watching scary movies.

I check my phone when *The Exorcist* is over and see it's almost three in the morning, so I decide to head to my room. Dad never changed it in hopes that I'd still frequent often so it looks the same as it did in high school. Luckily, I had a plain taste back then so I still feel at home in the beige room. I note the three missed calls and sixteen unread texts from Cayson. Yup, sixteen. All about the seating options the venue is offering. I wouldn't even think there would be that many ways to set up seats for eighty people. Turns out there totally is and I have the visuals in my texts to prove it. But he's excited and that's what matters. If arranging the chairs in a moon shape around the alter makes him happy, then so be it. And if it keeps my mom occupied, all the better.

I change into my oversize tee and my favorite silky sleep shorts and climb under the covers. I know I should be tired, but ironically I feel energized. I lay there with my eyes closed for all of five minutes before I give up knowing I'm not going to be able to fall asleep. There's only one thing that's going to help me unwind and go to sleep. I should feel weird about being in my childhood room in my dad's house, but I'm desperate for release.

I rummage through my duffle bag until I find what I'm looking for. Don't ask me why I brought my hot pink bullet vibrator on this trip, but I'm thanking past me for tossing it in there. Consider it a bedtime ritual of sorts. I know he's dreaming of buffet options by now but I decide to send Cayson a spicy text anyway. I don't do it often thanks to my lack of confidence where sex is concerned, but I'm feeling spicy. My alter ego Clarissa just gave advice to a girl who didn't know how to spice things up in her long distance relationship. Hello? Sexting exists for a reason. So taking my own advice, I shove my self-conscious thoughts to the back of my mind.

I prop my pillow up against the headboard and lay back as I pop my knees up and let my legs fall apart. My nipples harden against my silky tank top as they rub against the material. Silk always does something to me. I slip my hand down my shorts and feel my wetness. I angle the phone so that the camera gets a good shot of my cleavage, my hardened nipples, and my hand down my shorts. It's not a full on pornographic shot by any means but it'll do the job. When I finally get a picture that satisfies me, I pull up Cayson's text thread and hit send. He won't see it till morning, but who doesn't want to wake up to a sexy shot of their fiancée?

I toss my phone to the bed and lay back on the pillows. I turn the vibrator on low to stay quiet and slip it down my shorts pressing it firmly to my throbbing clit. It doesn't take me long to finish with a vibe so I only need a couple minutes. I close my eyes and bring my other hand to my throat, gently squeezing. I can feel myself quickly climbing to orgasm as I bite my lower lip and squeeze my eyes shut imagining my arms and legs being tied to the bed as a heavy hand squeezes the air from my throat. Moving my free hand from my throat and into my shorts I slip a finger inside my pussy, pumping quickly. I imagine myself being choked while my clit is teased. I'm so close, but I want to hold out a little longer. I find it erotic to be held back from climax. I'm totally lost in thought and pleasure when my phone dings.

I let out a groan of frustration as I reach for my phone and a wave of surprise hits me when I see Cayson's name on the screen. He's awake? That's strange for him. But that's good news for me. Phone sex would be great right now. Not that he and I have ever done it, but hearing a man moan through the phone would send me over the edge with how desperate I am for release. My blood starts to boil when I open his text and see his response. A question mark; that's it.

Did he seriously just send me a question mark like he's confused? Shouldn't a man be excited when they get a sexy picture from their woman? I don't feel like arguing so I opt for not responding. I think I need to talk to him about our sex life when I get back to Florida. I've been putting the conversation off hoping that it changes on it's own, but it's obvious my needs aren't being met and I can't expect him to know that when I refuse to acknowledge it, though it's not like I haven't tried. I turn the vibrator up one more notch and press it firmly to my clit so I can finish.

The orgasm doesn't give me the satisfaction I need, so I grab my laptop and pull up my column trying to come up with a response to my latest reader submission but come up empty handed slamming my laptop closed. Sometimes I wish someone close to me knew what I did for a living so I had someone to talk to about it.

In fact, nobody knows the details of my job. As far as anyone close to me is concerned, I work from home as a virtual assistant. I've always kept the details vague and changed the subject when the topic was brought up. It's not that I'm ashamed of what I do by any means, but I just don't feel like having that awkward conversation with my mother or my dad. I don't have any girl friends to talk to and Cayson would want to read the column to see what I'm writing about. Let's just say, he would not look at me the same if he knew what I fantasized about in the bedroom, or the advice that I was giving other women about vibrators and butt plugs. That man is as vanilla as vanilla comes. No chocolate drizzle, no sprinkles, no chocolate chips, not even a sugar cone. He is a single scoop of vanilla in a paper cup, but the expensive kind with the vanilla beans in it.

Don't get me wrong, I think there is a time and place for vanilla to be enjoyable, but for fucks sake sometimes I wish that man would fist my hair so tight he's practically ripping it from my scalp while he fucks me ruthlessly from behind not giving a damn that he's handling me like a rag doll. Then ideally his tender, gentle, loving side can come out to soothe the bruises after.

I know what you're thinking. I write sex advice columns for a living and I can't even talk to my fiancé about slacking in the bedroom. But it's more complicated than that. Every time I've tried to do something even slightly out of the norm for us in the bedroom, whether it be trying to ride him, dirty talk, extensive foreplay, the man seizes up. I don't even want to talk about the time I was dumb enough to try handcuffs. Never again. But after all, sex isn't everything, and I think I can survive a lifetime of plain Jane sex, even if Clarissa Rivers would beg to differ.

III

New Message

To thirstwithclarissa@gmail.com

Sex advice

Dear Clarissa,

My husband and I have been together for eight years. We have two kids together and our intimacy has become almost nonexistent. We only have sex about once a month and it is extremely boring vanilla sex. I've tried getting my husband to change positions, try toys, and increase the amount of sex we have. He just doesn't seem interested in changing. It makes me feel like he doesn't find me attractive. I need more in the bedroom but I don't know how to make him understand. What can I do?

Chapter 7
Tatum

It's after nine before I'm up and out of bed. I slip on my oversized hoodie, my stained ripped up jeans, and my old slippers. The smell of "Charlie's Crispier'n Hell Bacon" has me trudging my tired ass to the kitchen in search of breakfast and a cup of caffeine.

"Morning," Dad says as he sets a dirty dish in the sink.

"Good morning. Do I smell bacon?" I say through a yawn as I sit down at the kitchen island.

"Crisping up just the way you like it. I've got eggs going too, and I figured I would whip up those blueberry vanilla pancakes you used to love."

My eyes shoot up at the mention of the pancakes. Those were my favorite thing dad used to make me growing up. I begged for him to make them at least once a week.

"You didn't have to do all of this, Dad," I say as I get up to help by washing the dirty dishes. Dad has always been the type to clean as he goes, and I know he hates a dirty kitchen.

"I haven't seen you in two years, honey. I wanted to go all out. Besides, I'm sure you hardly ever get a decently cooked meal with how much you've been working lately, and we both know Cayden can't even boil a pot of water."

He's got me there. I like to cook, but I just don't have the time and Cayson can't cook to save his life. He tried microwaving raw chicken once, and we were both running for the toilet to hurl when we bit into the pink meat. We both live on the frozen pre-made meals and take-out at this

67

point. I can't lie that the idea of those pancakes has my mouth watering. I swear those things could make me orgasm on their own.

"Shit," Dad sighs running his palm over his tired face. "Bad news," he says as he opens the oven to check on the bacon before tossing the container of blueberries in the trash.

"What?" I ask, turning from the sink.

"These blueberries aren't any good. I thought I had more in here but I guess I don't. Damn it."

I can't help but get a little disappointed and he must see it on my face because he looks at me with hope in his eyes.

"Why don't you run to the store and grab another container? I'll throw the eggs in the microwave to keep them warm and the bacon won't be crispy enough for you for a while anyway."

I really don't want to run to the store, but I do have my heart set on those pancakes. I give him a shy smile as I dry off my hands and reach for his keys.

"You don't care if I take your truck do you?"

"Go ahead and take your brother's car," he says. "I've been having issues with the truck lately and don't want it to break down on you in town."

"I don't know why you still have that thing. It breaks down more than it runs. You've had it since I was a baby. Why don't you go buy a new one?"

"Actually, I've had it at least nine months before you were a baby," he winks. "Call it a sentimental attachment."

It breaks my heart that he's still holding on to the idea of Mom, but I let it go and grab Jace's keys.

"Speaking of my brother, is he still asleep?" Not that I really care. If I want to take his car, I'll take his car.

"Are you surprised?" Dad laughs. "He won't even know you took the car. By the time you get back, he'll still be out."

Dad pulls out his wallet shoving a five dollar bill in my hand before I head outside.

The cold breeze has me pulling my sweatshirt tighter. I'm halfway down the driveway when I realize that I should have changed before I left. I look in the rearview mirror and notice my hair is a frizzy mess up in a bun, and I have dark circles under my eyes that I didn't bother to cover up with concealer. I could go back inside and change, but I'm lazy. Not to mention I am starving and can only think about blueberry pancakes. I pull out of the driveway and decide it's not a big deal because I'll be in the store two minutes.

I take my time driving the trek into town, feeling reminiscent as I travel down the country roads, feeling a bout of anxiety when I pull into the Lucky's Foodliner parking lot, noting that it looks the exact same as it always has.

Two minutes later, I'm walking out of the front doors, blueberries in hand, with my head down, satisfied I didn't run into anyone I know when I hear someone say my name.

"Tatum? Oh my God! No way!"

I look up and am about to run into her as my brain registers who I'm looking at. Asher's sister Ari throws her arms around me in a tight hug before pulling away.

"Holy shit, girl," Ari says, looking me up and down. "I haven't seen you in forever. How are you? Did you move back? Oh it's so nice to see you."

Ari was always a nice girl, though she always ran a mile a minute and I can see she still does. We lost touch after I graduated and moved to Florida. She is three years younger than Asher and I, but I always figured she would have graduated and moved away to get out of our rinky dink town. The fact that she's looking at me as if nothing has changed makes my guilt fester for leaving her without explanation, but I always figured Asher filled her in, painting me to be the bad guy of the story.

I brush some stray hairs out of my face and give her a slight smile. There isn't the slightest hint of judgement in her eyes.

"Oh, no," I tell her. "I didn't move back. I'm just visiting my dad for the weekend and then heading back to Florida."

Before I can process what she's doing, she grabs my hand and pulls it closer to her as she lifts her sunglasses off her face to get a better look.

"Holy fuck! Now that is a rock. Damn girl, who did you bag? He must be a CEO or something with that kind of bling on your hand."

I told Cayson I wanted something unique and dainty, an antique with some history maybe, but he let my mom talk him into a two carat cushion diamond with a diamond band. Far more flashy than I would have picked, but he was proud of his choice.

I laugh and cringe at how nervous I sound. It's been years since I've spoken to anyone from my past and suddenly talking to Ari has me remembering about my time in this town.

"He's not a CEO, just has extravagant taste," I say, hiding the ring behind my back. My brain is telling me this girl should hate me for leaving her high and dry, the memory of promising her beach days in Florida flying to the front of my mind and the fact that she's acting like we're still friends hurts my heart. She was like a little sister to me.

"But anyway, how are *you*?" I ask to shift the conversation. "Do you still live here?"

"Yeah, I always planned on getting out of here, but I couldn't leave after I graduated. My fiancé wanted to stay here close to his family, and I didn't have the heart to go somewhere without him so we stayed put."

"Fiancé?" Now I'm looking at her hand for the bling. "Wow. I had no idea you were engaged. "

She proudly shoves her hand out in front of her, wiggling her fingers to show off the sparkle of the ring on her left hand. Rather than a diamond, hers is a beautiful blue gemstone that shines in the sunlight.

"It's nothing the size of yours, but I still love it," she beams. "I think the color suits me."

Her happiness is obvious as she stares at her ring admiring it like it's the first time she's seen it.

"It's beautiful, Ari. Congratulations, I'm so happy for you. I'm so sorry for how I left things. I should've–"

"Nope, not important," she interrupts. "I'm not mad at you if that's what you're thinking. You don't owe me an explanation. Anyway, speaking of fiancés, my engagement party is actually tonight. You have to come!"

I can feel the blood draining from my face as she finishes her sentence, a hopeful gleam in her eyes that I'm going to agree. I am not going to that party. No way in hell.

She must see my apprehension when she looks at me.

"Don't worry; he won't be there," she says. The tone of her voice tells me what I need to know.

I don't know what she thinks happened between Asher and me, but she must know it didn't end well.

"Your brother isn't coming to your engagement party? You two were always so close though."

I can sense her agitation as she says, "Yeah, we were. We still are but he thinks it's dumb that I'm getting married so young, and he said he didn't really have the time with everything he had going on. My mom said she tried talking him into it but she said he didn't seem very thrilled with the idea. You know how Asher is."

I don't anymore actually but I keep that thought to myself. Of course, if he's still fighting against marriage, maybe I do know how he is.

"If he says he'll think about it, then he's not coming," Ari says.

"I'm sorry. That's shitty of him. But I don't think I can make it either. I leave Sunday afternoon and I promised my dad that I'd spend all weekend with him and Jace."

I can tell she doesn't plan on letting me give her no as an answer.

"Oh come on!" she pleads. "It'll just be a couple of hours. There will be cocktails and food. I'll even let you take some cake back to your dad. I know he's a sucker for dessert."

She's not wrong. My dad can be bribed into just about anything if dessert is involved.

"Besides, like I said, Asher won't be there and you can meet my fiancé, Liam. It'll be fun. Come on, please? For old times sake?"

The optimism on her face is killing me. She's looking at me like Bambi with her fucking doe eyes. I sigh and and shift on my feet uncomfortably.

"I guess I can stop by for a little bit," I tell her. "But I don't have a gift for you. I'd feel shitty showing up without a gift."

"Bitch please, I just invited you. I don't expect a present. I invited like every extended family member I could think of so trust me, there will be plenty of gifts. I just want you there. It starts at seven. You remember where my parent's house is right?"

"Yeah, I remember." My voice just barely audible as memories in that house flash through my mind. How could I forget that house? I remember exactly where it is.

"Okay, I can't wait! I'll see you tonight!" she says as she dashes into the supermarket. I throw my stuff in the passenger seat of the car and drive back to the house. I don't know why I am so on edge about the fact that I agreed to go to Ari's party. I have missed her, and it will be nice to hang out with her again before I leave. I just can't seem to shake the uneasy feeling I have about it aside from the fact that I'm going to look like an asshole not bringing a gift to an engagement party.

I toss Jace's keys on the counter as I walk in the kitchen and see dad pulling out a tray of bacon perfectly crispy just like he promised. I plop the bag with the blueberries down on the island as Dad sets the hot pan down on the stove.

"Thank you, honey," he says. "I already made the batter so the pancakes will be done in no time."

"Thank you for this, Dad. I appreciate it. I'm gonna hop in the shower real quick."

I throw my sheets in the washer before heading to the bathroom and shed my clothes while I wait for the water to warm up. I grab my phone and see I missed a good morning text from Cayson earlier. I haven't replied to him since his awkward reply to my picture last night. It pissed me off though I know I'm partly to blame. I send a simple *Morning* and nothing else.

I quickly rinse off and hop out of the shower. I decide I'll take another one to shave and everything before I go to the party tonight, but right now I want my damn pancakes.

Chapter 8
Tatum

After I ate breakfast with Dad and took another shower, I asked him to take me to the boutique in town so I could get a dress for tonight. You would think with how much he begged me to come this weekend, he would have wanted to come with me. But instead he told me to ask Jace because he wanted to work on his truck. It seemed like there was more to his story but I let it go.

So now I'm in the passenger seat of Jace's car while he huffs and mumbles under his breath about taking me into town.

"Jace, I swear if you huff one more time, I'm punching you in the throat," I say as he scolds me from the driver's seat.

"Well, I'm sorry if I don't want to go dress shopping, Sis. It's not exactly my thing. Hey, I have an idea."

I already have a feeling I know where this is going before he finishes his thought.

"Why don't I invite Kara?"

"Jace, why would you invite your late night booty call? I thought she was the girl from two months ago. Besides, she doesn't even live here and I won't take that long anyway," I tell him as we turn onto the main street of our small town.

"I'll have you know, she's not just a booty call," he insists. "Besides, she could tell you what looks good."

"I'm not waiting forty minutes for your boo thang to drive here, and I've seen pictures of that girl. I have no interest in looking like a hooker tonight."

He glares at me but doesn't argue because he knows I'm right. Kara might be a nice girl, but I have yet to see a picture of her where her boobs aren't about to bust out of her shirt, or her ass isn't peeking out of her dress.

"Just drop me off and drive around town for a bit," I say. "Or go grab a coffee at Frothies and I'll text you when I'm done."

He pulls up to the curb of the boutique and I jump out of his car before he has a chance to protest. I throw him a *Love you* over my shoulder and laugh when I see he's flipping me off before he peels off down the street.

I've been in the shop all of three minutes before I'm worried I won't find anything I remotely like. Not to mention this boutique doesn't look like it carries anything above a size four, maybe six, let alone a size fourteen, and I don't really feel like spending eighty dollars on a dress for a party that I don't really want to go to. This boutique wasn't here when I was in school, but I know the owner's daughter and I'm not surprised by the price tags or the attitude that is radiating off the woman behind the counter.

"Can I help you find anything specific?" the woman asks.

"Um, do you have anything in bigger sizes?"

If I didn't know better, I would say the look she's giving me is a bit judgmental. Who am I kidding? The majority of this town is judgmental.

"We have a discount rack in the back corner over there," she smiles. "You might find something more suited for *you* over there."

Is she insinuating I'm poor *and* fat? If this wasn't the only place to buy a dress within thirty minutes I'd flip her off and walk out, but unless I want to show up tonight in an oversized Little Big Town tee, stained jeans, and sandals, I don't have a choice. And the Clemson house is not the type of place you show up wearing an outfit like that. The thought of her parents–do I call them Elizabeth and Mark?--has my stomach in knots because I've missed them, too. They were like a second set of parents to me, but after everything, I highly doubt they'll still treat me like I'm one of their own.

I walk over to the discount rack and flip through the few dresses hanging there. Surprisingly, they are in my size. I'm not going to comment on the irony that the bigger sizes are cheaper than the ninety dollar dresses at the front that take about three inches of fabric. I'm all for supporting small businesses, but who the fuck pays ninety bucks for a dress? I pick up a form fitting royal blue dress and head to the fitting room to try it on.

I pull the thick fabric curtain closed and slip off my jeans and top, sliding the dress over my hips. I'm pleasantly surprised when I turn to look in the mirror and like what I see. It falls a little higher than mid thigh with a small v shape cutout exposing some extra skin, and I can't deny that my ass looks incredible. It has a deep plunging neckline that shows off my cleavage just enough, and a low back. It's more revealing than I would typically go for but I feel like a sexy goddess. Luckily, I packed a pair of sandals that will look good with it. Clearly I was still in a Florida mindset when I packed because I'm going to freeze my ass off. I fucking hate Michigan with this stupid ass cold weather.

"Everything okay in there?" Judgy McBitchface asks.

I can hear the concern in her voice like she's either worried that I got stuck in the dress or I'm trying to steal it. I fucking hate that I love the dress so much. This bitch doesn't deserve my money. I grit my teeth trying to suppress the urge to rip the curtain open and smack her.

"Yeah, everything is fine. I'll be right out."

As I'm shimmying the dress off I hear my phone ding. Expecting a text from Jace complaining about how long I'm taking, I'm surprised when I see it's from Cayson. *I'm going to hang out with some buddies tonight so I won't be able to talk.*

I should probably question him about what buddies he's talking about. It should bother me that he doesn't seem obsessed with talking to me today like he has been, but I know I'm likely getting into my own head. I type out a quick *Ok. Have fun.* as I exit the fitting room and head to the counter where the woman still looks like my presence is repulsing her.

"Will this be all?" she says as she grabs the dress between her thumb and pointer finger like it's contaminated. It's illegal to murder people, Tatum. She's just a cunt with a shitty home life.

"Yup," I say with a tight lipped smile and wait for her to throw the dress in a bag and tell me the total.

"Forty-seven fifty please."

She cringes as I hand her my debit card and I can't help but laugh to myself. One of my girl friends from college ordered a sleeve for it as a joke gift for my twenty first birthday and I've kept it ever since. It's bright pink and has black script across it that says *I love cock.* I didn't even know you could get such a thing, but I won't deny I kind of love it. I especially love the look on the woman's face as she takes it from me to swipe it. She's appalled. Good.

She hands me a pen and the receipt to sign and I can't help but shoot her a dirty look. Since when are we supposed to tip retail workers? I make sure she sees me scribble zero on the tip line and sign my name with an X and O. I turn to leave and the urge takes over.

"Cunt," I mumble just loud enough for her to hear.

"What was that?" She asks with venom in her voice.

"C U next Tuesday!" I say hoping she understands my passive aggressive insult. I snatch the bag from the counter and walk out as I send

Jace a quick text to let him know I'm done. When he doesn't reply after a few seconds I check his location. He's at Frothies.

When I walk in I'm not as surprised as I should be to see him flirting with the cute blonde barista behind the counter.

"I'll have a medium iced chai please," I say and give Jace a knowing nudge.

He pulls out his wallet and hands her his card. He always buys my food when we're together.

"Thanks, baby. I'll pay you back later," I say and shoot him a wink. It's taking everything in me not to laugh out loud at the look on his face, and the heat climbing up his neck. The barista hands me my drink and tells us to have a good day, clearly irritated that Jace was hitting on her if he has a girlfriend.

"What the fuck was that?" Jace yells as we head to his car.

"Oh, don't be like that. You should be thanking me. I don't think Kara would approve of you hitting on that barista. Though I will say she was pretty. You two would make cute babies."

He scoffs like the idea disgusts him.

"What Kara doesn't know wont hurt her," he says. "Besides, I guarantee she's fucking other guys when she isn't fucking me so it's fine."

My eyebrows shoot up as I look at him.

"I thought she was more than just a booty call?"

"Shut up and get in the car."

I laugh and slide in my seat knowing he's not really mad at me. He may be in his idiotic man-whore stage, but we still love each other. If I didn't know he was doing well in school, I'd probably be a little more concerned for his well being.

"And don't ever refer to me as baby again," he says. "That's fucking weird."

"Got it, Daddy."

He peels out of the parking spot while I laugh and manage to pull a smirk from him.

Chapter 9

Tatum

◆

Dad was still tinkering with his truck when I left for the party, so I asked Jace if I could take his car. He said he would drop me off and pick me up later since he's meeting Kara tonight. If I didn't know better, I'd think he was getting attached to that girl.

As I walk up the steps of the house I remember all too well, I wonder if I made a bad choice deciding to come tonight. Opening the front door, I don't have the chance to second guess myself and call Jace to turn around to pick me up before Ari is throwing her arms around me in a hug.

"Oh, I'm so glad you came! I was worried you wouldn't show up. Get in here, I want to introduce you to my fiancé."

She pulls me through the front door into the main room, and I can smell the fruity liquor on her breath.

"You have to try this stuff. It's incredible!" she says as she hands me a glass full of whatever she's been drinking. "You can't even taste the alcohol."

I can tell by her giggling that she's clearly already indulged in a few of them and the party just started. But this party is about her, so she can do what she wants.

I take a sip of the vibrant drink and am pleasantly surprised by the fruity taste that covers my tongue. She was right. I can't taste any alcohol.

Taking a look around the room, I immediately feel anxious and out of place. It feels like I walked into a wedding reception. Of course the Clemson house has always been over the top stunning, but this is a whole new level. There are several tables placed methodically throughout the room where numerous guests are sitting, munching on tiny food. There's a sweetheart table at the back of the room, decorated in beautiful fresh flowers, and a table just to the right that is already overflowing with gifts. Her parents sit together at the front of the room, and their eyes are immediately drawn to mine as I put my hand up in an awkward wave. I can't tell if her mom recognizes me or not. The bar sits on the far right side of the room that is being manned by a beautiful specimen of a human being. I know where I'm going when I get a chance.

After a few minutes of talking with her and her fiancé, Liam, about how amazing Ari is and how he's not waiting a second to make babies with her, I take my glass and move to the corner of the busy room that she dragged me into. There's already a table filling up with gifts, so I feel less guilty that I came empty handed. Ari clearly pulled out every family contact she had. I can't say I blame her though. I guarantee a few of those gifts are worth more than my car.

I watch from the corner of the room as Ari greets every person who walks in the house, Liam at her side, his hand resting on the small of her back. She is far more bubbly than I could ever be, but I have missed her. She was always like the little sister I never had, and watching her float around the room has me missing our friendship. After college, I lost contact with most of my girl friends, so it's refreshing to have a familiar friendship back.

Watching her with Liam, I can tell she's beyond happy. She got the relationship I always wanted, and in a way I envy her for it. He can't keep his hands off of her, and I know if she saw the way he is constantly looking at her, she'd melt instantly. You know those scenes in romance movies where the guy watches her, clear admiration in his eyes? She looks at him like he is her entire world, and I don't doubt that he treats her the same, like she's everything he will ever need. Ari was never one to bargain with her happiness, so I have no doubts that she'd kick him to the curb for treating her as anything less than she's worth.

Half an hour later, the room is packed full of people I don't recognize, presumably Ari's family members from out of town. I always knew they had a large family, but most of them lived in different states so I never met them. I'm not complaining though because I've been able to get away with hiding in the corner to myself nursing the same drink I started on when I got here. I still don't have the courage to go talk to Elizabeth and Mark.

I'm not much of a drinker anymore. I used to enjoy a casual glass of wine or amaretto sour on the weekends, but Cayson isn't a drinker so I don't indulge in alcohol often anymore. I've smiled politely at a few people who made eye contact, but I've managed to avoid a lot of conversation which is fine with me. My social battery isn't charged right now.

Ari's mom ushers her over to the table to open her gifts. I don't pay much attention as I hear a door shut until I see Ari jumping from her chair and running to the doorway.

"I can't believe you made it!" she says as she latches onto the person standing in the doorway.

It takes my brain a few seconds to realize what I'm looking at. What the actual fuck. This isn't happening. I'm going to need another drink.

Chapter 10
Asher

Ari runs and latches onto me faster than a damn squirrel.

"I can't believe you made it!" she says as she stands on wobbly legs. Someone has clearly had a few drinks.

"I didn't think I could get away," I tell her. "But I managed to get the weekend off."

I can tell she really is happy to see me. I'm happy to see her, too. It's been too long since I've seen my little sister. I am already starting to regret my decision to come back when I see how many of our extended family members Ari invited, some of whom I know I haven't seen since I was in diapers.

Not that I blame her. I'm sure the gifts she's getting out of it are well worth the two hours she has to talk to them. I am definitely not in the mood for socializing so I plan to say as little as possible and leave as quickly as I can without getting scolded by my mother or my sister for not extending my stay. They're already mad that I didn't come to Thanksgiving dinner last night. Though the slurring of my sister's words has me confident I'll be able to slip out without her caring. She's such a lightweight.

"Come on," she orders. "I was just about to open some gifts. Do you want a drink?"

"Is that even a question?" If I'm going to deal with this party, then I'm going to need a drink in my hand.

She leads me over to the bar and I ask the bartender for a whiskey neat. Apparently that isn't on the menu from the mother of the bride so I have to settle for a beer instead. If I wasn't driving I would be working my way to getting wasted. Social events are not my thing.

"You can sit at the table up front with Mom and Dad. I told them not to save you a seat because I didn't think you'd show up, but I think Mom saved you one anyway. Oh, and I should probably warn you–"

"Ari, get over here and open your gifts!" My mom shouts from the front of the room. "You have guests waiting."

Just as I'm about to ask what she needs to warn me about, Ari turns on her heel running directly towards her fiancé waiting at the gift table. I've met him a few times, but I still can't remember his name. He seems to treat her well though so I guess that's all that matters. I turn away from the bar and make my way to the table where my mother is waiting for me with a look of loving shock on her face.

Ten minutes later I've lost count of how many gifts Ari has opened, but my beer is gone and I need something else to drink. Of course our small ass town doesn't have Uber, and I'm driving the old beater that I bought to keep here when I visit so I guess I'm going nonalcoholic for the rest of the night. I may break a lot of rules and test boundaries, but drinking and driving isn't one of them. Damn, I sound like a public service announcement.

As I make my way back over to the bar, I see something that catches my attention. A tight little blue dress on beautifully luscious curves. I can't see her face because she's facing the bartender, but with those curves, and an ass like that, I have a feeling I'm going to like whatever I see in the front. It's been too damn long since I've fucked anyone, and the sight of this woman's ass has my cock jerking to life behind my zipper.

Granted, chances are pretty high that she went to school with my sister, and Ari will flip a lid if I sleep with any of her friends, but I've got to see the rest of this girl. The back of her dress falls teasingly low, just above the top of her gorgeous ass. I make my way over and wave the bartender over for a water.

"So," I say, all smooth, still looking down at the bar "How do you know Ari?" I've never been one to struggle with confidence, but something tells me I'll struggle finding my words once I see her face.

"I don't," she says without turning around. "I'm actually just crashing the party for the free booze."

Why the fuck does that voice sound so familiar? Finally, she turns, and as I look up at the woman standing next to me, familiar eyes staring back at me, my blood runs cold.

"Tate." I can hear my brain telling me to move, to say something more than her name, but my body is frozen.

"Sure is. In the flesh," she says as she gulps down another drink, signaling for another.

"I uh…" Fucking hell, formulate a damn sentence, man. I don't know why her presence is throwing me off so much. And of course she looks fucking phenomenal because why wouldn't she? Why would I expect the woman I loved for years would have run off and deteriorated into something hideous?

Her blonde hair is in waves swept over one of her shoulders. I can't help my eyes from trailing down her body. And my god those curves. Her thigh is sticking out from the small slit in her gown, and my traitorous dick is trying to show its approval.

"I didn't know you'd be here," I say as I force my eyes back up to her face.

She's already halfway through the drink she just ordered. Clearly, I'm not the only one flustered by this meeting.

"That makes two of us," she says. "It wasn't really planned out, just a last minute thing. I'm visiting my dad for the weekend, and I ran into Ari this morning. She pretty much demanded I be here, though seeing how tipsy she already is, I'm not sure she'll even remember I came. Meaning this was all pointless."

The last sentence is barely above a whisper and I don't think she even meant for me to hear it, but I know exactly what she means. It's obvious she didn't want to come, and she definitely didn't think I would be here. I can tell she's looking everywhere but at me, and it's pissing me off.

"Anyway, I'm gonna get back to my seat," she says over her shoulder as she walks away with a new drink in hand. "Nice seeing you."

Nice seeing me? What the fuck?

Chapter 11

Asher

◦◆◦

I don't care that she isn't happy to see me, because I'm not happy to see her either (though my cock tells a much different story). I don't care that she looks so fucking beautiful. I don't care that she got the last word. Did she seriously just act like nothing ever happened between us? As if she wasn't the love of my life. As if it hasn't been eight years since she disappeared without a word after graduation.

Fine, I do care. She doesn't get the last word. That's not how this is going to happen. If she wants to pretend that I never meant anything to her, that's fine. I'll play her game, but she isn't going to like how I win.

My sister is still opening the absurd amount of gifts by the time I make it back to my seat with my parents. My mom plants a kiss on my cheek telling me how much she's missed me, droning on about something, but I'm not tuned in to what she's saying. My gaze is locked on *her*. I can tell by the way she's fidgeting and slightly swaying in her chair that she's almost drunk. She hasn't looked my way one time which tells me that she's more bothered by my presence than she cares to let on, but I'm going to make her show it. I can feel the anger radiating from my body as she dares to look in my direction. She must not like what she sees because she immediately looks away and goes back to sipping her drink.

As I get up to make my way to her, I feel a hand on my arm.

"Hey, you," the woman says as she flirtatiously rubs her hand up and down my arm. It takes me a second to realize who it is I'm looking at: Shauna Fucking Gates. Why the fuck she's here, I haven't a clue. She's a year younger than me, and I don't remember her ever being friends with my sister, though the attention whore she is, it wouldn't surprise me if she hadn't actually even been invited.

She had a huge thing for me in high school, but I never let it go anywhere after a quick hookup the summer before junior year. Other than being a quick fuck, nothing about her interested me. She was always boring and incredibly predictable, and did I mention attention whore?

Tatum always hated her because even after we got together, Shauna still made it clear she had gotten what Tate had first. Shauna was known for fucking guys who had girlfriends, and when she couldn't get that from me, it pissed her off.

"Hey," I say with the intention of leaving it at that and leaving her standing there. That is until I look over and see Tate staring right at me with Shauna's hand on my arm. She was never good at hiding her emotions, and clearly that hasn't changed much. When she sees me making eye contact with her she looks away. It might make me a total douchebag, but I'm going to win her game, so I play right into Shauna's hand.

Returning her smile, I allow my gaze to travel down Shauna's body making sure to be obvious about it. I let my eyes linger on her boobs longer than a respectful guy would to make sure she catches me. When I look back at her face I see it clearly worked because she's blushing and licking her lips that are doused in far too much lip gloss. Nothing about her try hard appearance is attractive to me, but she doesn't need to know that. I can feel eyes on me as I talk to Shauna, but I don't allow myself to look at the woman staring in my direction. As far as she needs to know, I plan on fucking Shauna as soon as the chance presents itself.

"So how long are you home?" she asks as she fidgets with her top, clearly trying to push the cleavage out more than it already is. "I haven't seen you in ages." This woman couldn't try any harder to flirt with me.

"I'm only home for the weekend," I deadpan. I'm finding it difficult to make myself have a conversation with her when I know she's already fucking me in her mind. My lack of enthusiasm doesn't seem to deter her though. Her desperation seeps from her makeup-heavy eyes.

"Oh, that's too bad. Maybe we can hang out after the party," she says as she traces circles on my chest with her bright blue acrylic nails. "We can go back to my place." The color causes my dick to jerk back to life as it brings back the picture of Tate in the same colored gown. I hate that I can't stop thinking about her.

Shauna's voice jerks me out of my head as she moves in closer. Everything about this conversation is repulsing me, and I desperately want it to end, and when I look up to see Tate walking out of the room into the hallway, it gives me the perfect opportunity.

"You know, I'm actually really tired from the flight, so I'm just gonna crash afterwards. Thanks for the offer."

I remove her hand from my arm and see her smile fall from her face, clearly frustrated. I guess tonight is my lucky night for pissing people off. Leaving her there, I make my way out into the hallway.

Most of the house is locked up so there's not many places she could have run to. It's not long before I find her out on the balcony right off the main living room. Her back is to me, and it's obvious she doesn't know I'm standing behind her as she sighs and runs her hands over her face before finishing off what is left in her glass. I don't know how many she had before I got here, but I know she's had at least four. Not that I've been paying that much attention to her. She rubs her hands up and down her arms clearly getting cold as she puts her hands on the railing and leans down, shoving her ass out. If I didn't know any better, I'd think she was trying to put on a show for me.

"Fuck," she sighs just barely above a whisper.

Shit, I should not be looking at her ass. Or thinking about the fact that with the way she's bent over, I can barely make out the outline of her thong, and my brain is picturing the way she'd feel, the way she'd scream my name as I took her from behind, gripping her hair in my fist as I left marks down her neck with my teeth. Fuck. And I definitely should not be adjusting myself in my pants. I linger there just watching her, not wanting to move, but not wanting to stay either. I don't get the chance to sneak out before she turns.

"Shit! Fucking hell!" she yells, dropping her empty glass.

She jumps, clutching her hand to her chest when she turns around and sees me standing feet away. Curses coming from that sweet little mouth of hers was never a thing in high school, but I have to say she's sexy as sin cussing like a sailor. Her words are slightly slurred from the alcohol she keeps chugging down.

I smile slightly, enjoying her reaction to my presence. Only until I see the splotchy redness on her face and the slight mascara smudges under her eyes. Then my smile falls. She's been crying, and it doesn't take a genius to guess why. I wanted to piss her off, so why am I so affected by seeing her tear-stained face?

"What? Why are you in here?" she snaps at me.

Suddenly whatever affectionate emotion I was feeling towards her is stomped out by my rising anger.

"Why are *you* in here?" I say as I inch closer to her.

"It was getting claustrophobic in there. I wanted some air. I got enough."

She goes to move around me, moving her body as far from me as possible, but I shift to the side blocking her.

"Excuse me," she says through gritted teeth.

She tries to move around me again, but I shift in front of her blocking her path yet again.

"What's your fucking problem?" she barks. "Move."

This time when she tries to get around me I feel myself grabbing for her arm before I realize what I'm doing.

She whips around staring at me with daggers and tears mixing in her eyes.

"What's wrong?" I ask her sympathetically even though I'm still fucking mad at her. I don't know why I'm even asking as if I care about her emotional well-being.

"Nothing," she says as she wipes the makeup from under her eyes, sniffling slightly.

"Clearly. What is it with women giving stupid answers to questions as if men haven't learned that *nothing* or *fine* are blatant lies?" I huff.

That seems to just push her buttons even more.

"First of all, men haven't learned shit. Secondly, maybe we wouldn't give stupid answers if the people asking them weren't asking questions they don't want to hear the answers to."

The pain in her voice is evident, but so is the anger.

"Isn't Shauna missing you?" she hisses.

This time I can't hide the smirk that tugs at my lips. She's jealous. So it worked. I don't know why I feel compelled to keep pissing her off, but the words are leaving my lips before I can talk myself out of it.

"She is," I say. "She's got an empty bed waiting for us at her place."

With that idiotic comment, she rips her arm out of my grasp and scoffs as she walks away. Instantly I regret what I said when I hear her trying to suppress a sob as she leaves the room. I can't get my feelings in check with this girl and it's confusing the hell out of me. I'm supposed to hate her for leaving like she did. I *do* hate her. Don't I? I knew she was going to be home this weekend, but her unexpected appearance at the party is making it hard to think straight.

I make my way back to the party and give Ari and her fiancé–what the fuck is that guy's name?--my congratulations again before giving my mom and dad a hug on the way out. I don't miss the comment my mom makes about coming home more often and making them a priority, but I decide to table that conversation. She makes sure to make me feel guilty for not staying at the house before I leave. It's the same routine every time I come home to visit. I know I have gotten bad about coming home to visit lately, but I don't have the energy to feel guilty about it. I'm itching to leave this party. But even more, I find I'm itching to see a particular blonde before I leave.

IV

To thirstwithclarissa@gmail.com

Relationship advice

Dear Clarissa,

My ex-boyfriend and I have been broken up for eight months. I'm still not over him, but today I saw him with the girl that he always told me not to worry about. I want to move on but I don't know how to when I'm still in love with him. How can I get over it?

Chapter 12
Tatum

Why the fuck did I come to this party? I should have stayed at Dad's and worked on my column, or kept him company while he worked on his truck. But no, I came here and look where it got me, exactly where I didn't want to be. With him.

I should say bye to Ari before I leave, but my brain is fuzzy from all the alcohol and I just want to get home to sleep it off. I knew it was a bad idea to come home. Everything that could have gone wrong did go wrong. I wasn't supposed to get jealous of Shauna "the boyfriend fucker" Gates on his arm. I shouldn't care if he fucks her… again. Asher isn't mine anymore and hasn't been for eight years. He can fuck whoever he wants, whore or not.

Of course she'd be all over him. He looks just as good as he did eight years ago, if not better. No, actually most definitely better. I hate myself for noticing how good he looked in his long sleeve dress shirt, his dark curls falling softly on his forehead. And those fucking eyes. Those green eyes that stare holes straight through my soul, like he can see my thoughts. He always could read me like an open book. Even as he shot dirty looks my way, I couldn't stop wanting his eyes to stare at me, though it's obvious his hatred for me is pretty fucking strong. Not that I should care how he feels about me. He has every right to be angry, but that doesn't mean I'm going to sit here and let him treat me like gum on the bottom of his shoe.

More importantly, I'm about to get married. Fuck. Cayson. Why am I out here crying over a guy that isn't my fiancé? I'm such a bitch. Maybe there was some truth to the small town gossip about me back in the day. Thank God Cayson's busy with friends tonight because I couldn't stomach a phone call with him. Literally or figuratively. I feel like I'm about to puke up the seven cocktails I've consumed in the last two hours. My dumbass didn't even stop to consider what a lightweight I've always been with alcohol.

As I'm walking out the front door clutching my purse to my chest and unsteadily walking down the front steps, I remember how much I fucking hate Michigan winters. I'm freezing, but luckily the alcohol lessens the cold.

I should just go back in the house to wait for my brother to come get me, but I'm not going back in there with *him*. I'd rather stand out here and freeze my tits off than go back in there and see his arrogant ass. I scrounge through my purse looking for my cell phone to call Jace to come pick me up. When it goes straight to voicemail, I'm ready to beat his face in when he gets here.

I call again. Voicemail. Stupid fucker must have turned his phone off while he's balls deep in Kara or the Frothies girl. Well, shit.

Looking at the time, I see it's almost eleven which means Dad is in bed. Even if I wanted to call him, he wouldn't hear his phone. That man sleeps like the dead. Guess I'm walking home, which is only a mere ten miles from here. Or is it five? Three? I can't fucking think straight. Regardless, Jace isn't going to stop his booty call to come pick me up, and I'm not asking anyone in that house to take me home. Luckily I'm in sandals, not heels. If I don't freeze to death by the time I get home, I am killing Jace.

I start walking down the sidewalk cursing under my breath when I hear footsteps behind me. My pulse picks up in warning as I clutch my phone in my hand. If living in Florida taught me nothing else, I definitely learned to be alert for tweaked out assholes. Subconsciously I know who it is, but my brain is telling my body that there's some Miami meth head behind me, and frankly I think I'd rather that be the case.

"Where are you going?" the meth head yells.

I turn around to see Asher standing on the steps of the house watching me. He looks ridiculously hot in his long coat, blowing on his hands to keep them warm. Shut the fuck up, Tatum; no he doesn't.

"Uhh, home."

"You're kidding right?" he says, coming toward me. "You can't drive. You're clearly drunk from the six glasses of whatever that fruity shit was."

I scoff. "Actually, I had seven glasses of *that fruity shit*. And I never said I was driving."

He looks around clearly looking for someone waiting to take me home. The dead and dark street makes it obvious there's no one waiting for me. Without saying anything else, I turn around and start walking down the sidewalk holding myself to keep as warm as possible, cursing myself for not wearing a coat because it would look stupid with my dress. I grumble when I hear his footsteps continuing behind me.

"You are not seriously walking home."

I don't turn around as I shout, "Sure am," though my voice is shaky both from the alcohol and the cold.

"Are you fucking serious, Tate? Are you forgetting that you live like ten miles out of town? Or the fact that it's dark and snowing. You're not walking home by yourself."

Ahh, so it is ten.

"That's where you're wrong, buddy. I'm a big girl, and nothing bad happens here anyway," I say, my toes already hardening into ice. "I'll be fine," I say, over my shoulder, throwing my arms out as if I'm enjoying the weather. "Besides, I like the cold air. It clears my brain, feels good in my lungs."

"For fucks sake, Tate, I'll drive you home."

"No thanks, I'm good," I say as I keep walking. The idea of heat in a car sounds phenomenal right now, but I am not getting in a car with that arrogant asshole and listening to him gripe about my presence being a disturbance.

"Tatum, I swear to God, just let me drive you," he says.

"Hmm. Let me think about it. Nope."

At that moment, as if the universe has been listening to us, the light flurry of snow picks up to a thick white blanket in the air and I lose my footing on a small patch of ice. I fall hard on my ass, but instead of yelling or crying, I laugh. I know it's the liquor making me laugh because that's going to hurt like a bitch in the morning. Ask a girl why she hopes her ass aches in the morning, it is definitely not from falling on the fucking ice.

Asher rushes to help me up, but I push his arm away not wanting him to touch me.

"Fucking hell, Tate," he says, grabbing at my arms, "You're drunk."

Still laughing, I have to calm myself to look at him. "No, I'm tipsy, not drunk."

I'm totally drunk.

"Why do you care anyway?" I ask, the ice soothing my ass. "You've been shooting me death glares all night. Your date is inside just waiting to fuck your brains out. I'll be on my way so you can get laid."

He mumbles something under his breath that I can't quite make out as he grabs me by the waist and hauls me up to my feet.

I choose to ignore the heat that warms my body from the touch of his fingertips on my arm. The tingles that run down my spine at the familiar feeling.

"Hey!" I yell.

I can't put up much fight before he has me steadied, holding on to me as his eyes bore into mine almost like he's searching for something.

"I have not been shooting you death glares all night," he says.

"Yes, you have! Every time you'd look in my general direction, you looked like you were ready to kill. Just leave me alone and I'll figure it out."

I can't prevent the tear slipping down my cheek. Though if it's because I'm upset about Asher, the stupid fucking freezing cold weather, or being stranded by my brother I'm not entirely sure.

"Well, it's not like I was expecting to see you here," he says. "It's been eight years. I was thrown off by–"

Still a bit unsteady on my feet, he grabs my wrist to balance me. It isn't until I follow his gaze to my ring that I understand why he stopped mid sentence. Without thinking I pull my hand behind by back really wishing I had been smart enough to wear a coat so I could stuff my hands in pockets right now.

"Yeah," I say. "Eight years." Taking a few steps back I look everywhere but at his face. "Anyway, tell your sister I said congratulations again, and uh, good luck with everything. I won't be making it to the wedding."

Before he can say anything else, or I'm stupid enough to let him see me cry again, I turn around and start walking as fast as my shivering body will carry me. I know I can't walk all the way home without getting hypothermia or passing out, so I keep walking as I pull out my phone to call Jace again. Straight to voicemail. *Fucking bastard.* Walking it is.

✝

I hear an engine approaching beside me. Clenching my chattering teeth I close my eyes hoping I don't hear it stop next to me.

"Get in the fucking car, Tatum. Don't make me throw your ass in the passenger seat."

When I don't move to get in the car, he throws it in park, cursing under his breath.

"It's freezing out here and the snow is picking up," he warns. "In that outfit you'll either be dead from hypothermia or kidnapped within ten minutes. Get. In. The. Car."

He makes sure to emphasize every word trying to intimidate me, as if he has any control over me anymore.

"Why do you care if I get kidnapped or die?" Honestly being kidnapped sounds better than having this conversation with him.

"Because I don't want to be a suspect if you go missing, or freeze to death, or some shit."

I don't plan on caving until I see him undo his seatbelt. He wasn't kidding about throwing me in the car himself, and while my body is betraying me by craving the warmth of his touch again, my brain is in fight or flight mode, and I don't have the energy for flight.

"Fine," I mutter through my chattering teeth and plop down in the passenger seat.

He rolls up the window and the feeling of the heat blasting through the vent is so heavenly I'm frozen in warm bliss, some of the tension falling off my shoulders.

"Buckle up," he says with irritation in his voice.

I'm too busy trying to get the feeling back in my fingers to care about a seat belt. Apparently, he doesn't care because two seconds later he's reaching over the center console buckling it for me. We both tense up when the action gets his face entirely too close to my cleavage.

He throws himself back into his seat turning the heat up even higher as he puts the car in drive.

"God, you'd think you're my boyfriend or something," I say, not looking at him.

I can hear him scoff under his breath.

"Yeah, well, where's your *husband*? He should be the one making sure you get home safe, not me."

If I wasn't so cold I would probably put more thought into the way he said the word *husband* as if it was bile on his tongue.

"*Fiancé,* and he's not here. I came back here by myself. Jace was supposed to pick me up but apparently he's more worried about getting his dick wet than taking me home so he turned his phone off."

"Why?" He looks at me as he pulls up to a stop sign. With how slow he's going on these roads, it probably would be faster for me to walk. Granted, I can tell it's getting icy but still.

"Probably because he's a teenage boy who has few ambitions besides fucking." I snap.

"No, why did you come back by yourself?"

"Because I wanted to. I'm a big girl now in case you forgot. I can do what I want."

Even as the words are leaving my mouth I can hear the venom in my voice. I'm angry but I don't know why I'm so mad. So he gave me dirty looks all night. I shouldn't care; I *don't* care. I should be grateful he didn't leave me in the cold. So what if he's planning on fucking Shauna. Then it hits me.

"Wait. What about Shauna?"

He looks at me as if it was a dumb question.

"What about her?"

Now I'm looking at him like he's the dumb one.

"Well, you said you were going back to her place," I tell him. "If you think for one second I'm going to sit in the car while you get your jollies off with her–"

"Will you shut the fuck up? I'm not going to her place. I never was."

Relief floods me at his admission. He's staring out the windshield clearly thinking something but not wanting to voice it. He should be thinking about putting his foot on the gas pedal since we're still sitting at the same stop sign.

"Then why did you say you were?"

Ignoring my question, he turns to me.

"Why are you marrying him if you don't even want to bring him home with you?" he asks. "Does he not like your dad or something? Is he too busy to make your family a priority?"

The word *home* feels wrong when talking about this town now because it hasn't been that for me in a very long time. I'm starting to regret getting in the car with him. I'll take my chances in the blizzard. His gaze right now is colder than the snow outside.

"I never said I didn't *want* to bring him with me," I say, pulling my knees up to my chest.

"You never said you wanted to either."

When I don't respond, he continues.

"Why *are* you marrying him then?"

"Why does anyone marry anyone? Because he's good to me!" I shout louder than I anticipated. His questions are getting under my skin and it's making me uncomfortable, though I'm not sure I even know why.

"So you're marrying him because he's good to you. Not because he makes you happy?"

"You better hope a cop doesn't pull up behind you," I grumble. "You've been sitting at this stop sign for ten minutes."

Clenching his jaw, he finally puts his foot on the gas and turns on his turn signal.

"So dramatic," he says under his breath. "You didn't answer all of my question."

"Where are we going?" I ask when he takes a right. "This isn't how you get to my house. You were supposed to go straight."

He doesn't answer me, or even acknowledge that I asked a question.

"Hello?" I say, leaning towards him and speaking louder, waving my hands. "Where. Are. We. Going?"

This time he glances in my direction but continues driving in silence. Huffing, I position myself until I'm pointing towards the window.

"Asshole," I mumble under my breath.

"Stubborn ass," He says, *not* under his breath.

I was in the mood to fight, but now I'm just in the mood to get out of this fucking car. He pulls into a parking lot at snail speed and parks in what I'm assuming is supposed to be a parking spot. The snow has picked up so much that the entire lot is in a thin blanket of white.

Taking in my surroundings I realize we're at a small apartment complex. It wasn't here when I lived in town, so it must be new.

Before I get the chance to ask, he speaks.

"Why did you do it?"

He's staring out the windshield like it would kill him if he looked in my direction.

"Do what?" I can sense that he's getting angry.

"You know what, Tate! Why the fuck did you disappear on me after graduation? We were best fucking friends, and then we have a fight and you just take off without saying anything? No goodbye, nothing. You just take off and leave for eight years without reaching out once. Who the fuck does that?"

My heart sinks. He's angry, but he's hurt too. I knew I probably hurt him when I left, but I didn't think he would have held onto the hurt for this long, not like I have.

Turning away from him I ask, "What are we doing?" But it comes out just barely above a whisper.

"Answer the question."

I can tell by the tone in his voice that he's not going to let it go. So I say the best thing that comes to my hazy mind: "There was no point in staying." I suck in a breath and lean my head back on the headrest to look out the window at the heavy snow. "You had your life plans and I had mine. We wouldn't have worked. We were on two totally different paths."

I can't control the emotion in my voice as I wipe away the tears that are forming in my eyes. He doesn't need to know the entire truth about why I left. It won't do anyone any good, and I swore he'd never find out. My answer isn't the complete truth, but it's also not a lie. It's the best I can give him.

"So all those years of friendship meant nothing to you? You didn't care that you were just throwing that all away?" His words were burning deeper than I wanted them to.

"Take me to my dad's, Asher," I say with a defeated sigh, trying to keep my voice from breaking.

With an angry huff he opens his door and walks to my side of the car to open mine.

"What are we doing? Where are we? I don't remember this being here," I say while staying planted in my seat, already missing the heat from the car vents.

"That's because it's new," he says, the warm car getting colder by the second. "I'm guessing you haven't been back to visit for a while."

His statement has me questioning how he knows I haven't been back here and hate that my heart flutters at the idea of him looking for me when he's home.

"They built it a couple of years ago," he says, standing with his hand on the door like he's waiting for me to get out.

"Okay, and what are we doing here?" I say, not budging. "You said you were taking me home."

I can't help the irritation in my voice. I want to go back to Dad's and pass out in my bed and forget this night even happened. This pit stop of his is just prolonging that.

"You're staying with me tonight."

My eyebrows shoot to my hairline.

"Like hell I am," I say, the cold from the winter breeze starting to freeze me again.

"Tate, you're drunk and the roads are getting bad. Your dad lives out in the country where the roads are going to be even worse. You are staying with me tonight and I'll drive you home in the morning once the roads are clear. Now get out of the car. It's fucking freezing out here."

"No. Why are we here anyway? We just left your parents' house."

He's clearly getting annoyed with me as he says, "Yes, but I'm staying *here*."

Unease hits me as I realize it might be his girlfriend's apartment. He said he wasn't going home with Shauna, but that doesn't mean he doesn't have a girlfriend.

"With who?"

He must realize I don't plan on getting out of the car any time soon so he climbs back in the driver's seat slamming his door, not turning on the engine. Pansy can't handle the cold.

"I'm staying by myself," he says, rubbing his legs. "It's my apartment."

Confused, I turn to look at him.

"Why do you have an apartment? Your sister said you still live in San Diego."

"I did. I do, but I rented this place out when it opened to have somewhere to stay when I come visit. I don't exactly enjoy staying in my childhood bedroom in my parent's house at twenty-six years old."

I can tell by his demeanor he's growing tired of the conversation, but I don't care. I'm not going in there with him.

He lets defeated silence fill the air, and my mind starts drifting with pictures of going inside with him. Alone. Memories of us in bed infiltrate my head as I remember the chemistry we had together. That night in his truck starts playing through my mind and the memory of his touch on my body is so vivid I can almost feel it. The way his hands desperately grabbed at my dress to expose my nipples as he took one into his mouth. The way his length pressed against my center through his jeans as I fought for more friction. The way his tongue invaded my mouth, greedily taking what he wanted as his fingers slipped under my dress before slipping into my slick heat, sending me over the edge as I came.

"What are you thinking about over there?"

His voice snaps me back to reality as I curse myself for letting my brain go where it definitely shouldn't.

I look at him feigning innocence and ignorance. "What? I'm just tired."

"Do you always rub your thighs together like that and moan when you're tired?"

I can feel the heat traveling up my neck at his words.

"I was not moaning," I say. Please tell me I wasn't fucking moaning from a daydream about my ex in front of him. By the ache between my thighs, I'm sure I totally fucking was.

He suddenly turns sharply to look at me.

"What do you mean *still* live in San Diego?"

"What are you talking about?" I ask.

"You said my sister told you I *still* live in San Diego. That would insinuate you already knew I lived there and considering I moved *after* you left and we haven't spoken since, how did you know where I lived?"

Panic sets in my gut as I search for a response. Damn this liquor for making my brain so slow. If I were in my right mind I'd be able to explain that I remember his mom telling me about San Diego. But instead all I can think of is the fact that I cyber stalked him over the years and knew that's where he landed long term. In my defense, I haven't looked him up in two years.

When I come up empty handed for a response, his mouth curls into a smirk as he looks at me.

"Must have been a lucky guess," he says as if he won something.

Then he casually opens his door and gets out, walking his smug ass toward the apartment building.

"I'm not staying here, Asher," I yell through the windshield. "I'll get my dad to pick me up."

I know damn well I won't be able to get ahold of him, but I'll say anything to keep Asher from getting his way.

"I already texted your dad and told him I'd be bringing you home in the morning," he yells without turning around. "I know he's probably asleep, but he'll see it when he wakes up."

I push open the car door and step onto the frozen parking lot.

"What the fuck is wrong with you?" I yell after him. "How do you even still have his number?" This fucker is going to make me go in that apartment.

"It doesn't matter," he says, still walking. "I have it, and I already texted him."

"I'm not having sex with you if that's what you're after," I say, catching up to him.

I glare at him. When he doesn't answer right away, I realize what he's looking at. My eyes follow his gaze straight to my peaked nipples poking through my dress. Fucking Michigan weather. I throw my arms around myself trying to hide them and warm myself up.

Clearing his throat when he realizes I caught him staring, he turns around to walk inside. Reluctantly, I follow.

"First of all," he says, digging in his coat pocket to pull out his keys and unlock the door, "If you think I'd have sex with you while you're drunk then you never knew me at all. Secondly, I don't want to sleep with you. It's pretty obvious you hate me. For what reason I don't know considering you have no reason to hate me, but whatever. I should be the one that hates you. And I only stick my dick in girls who *want* to fuck me. So unless you fall into that category, you're safe."

He gestures for me to go in first, looking at me as if waiting for me to clarify that I *do* in fact fall into that category.

Looking around his dark, empty apartment, I ask, "Then why am I here, Asher? Why am I in *your* apartment where *you* are forcing me to stay because *you* wouldn't let me walk home."

"Because despite what you think," he says, turning to look at me. "I'm not a complete dick."

"I never said you were."

"No, you're right," he says, hanging his coat in an otherwise empty closet. "You just said I was an asshole. And you've certainly been acting like you believe that."

"It's not like you've been the nicest to me all night either."

Suddenly I feel like a child arguing about who's right.

I'm obviously not getting to take my hot shower and pass out in my own bed tonight so I walk deeper into the apartment. When he flips on the light switch, I take in the space. It's almost completely bare. There's a small tv mounted on the wall, a brown futon, and a coffee table with a couple of magazines, what looks like a textbook, a pad of sticky notes, and a few pencils. There are no decorations, no throw pillows on the couch, or pictures on the walls. From here I can see a small kitchen that looks as if it could hold about three people before it got crowded.

"I'll take the couch and you can have my bed," he says.

"Ew. I'd rather have the couch," I say, unable to hide the repulsion in my voice.

"You didn't mind sleeping in my bed before," he says with a stupid smirk plastered on his face as he leans against the wall looking at me.

"Call that stupid teenage hormones. I don't want to sleep in the bed that you've jacked off and fucked other girls in."

109

The smirk falls from his face turning into a slight frown.

"And what would you say if I told you that I haven't fucked anyone in that bed?"

"I wouldn't believe you," I say folding my arms over my chest.

"Well you don't have to. I won't lie to you about the jacking off though."

"You're disgusting."

He's smiling and I hate how good he looks. His long sleeve black button down dress shirt looks ridiculously good on him, and it's obvious he still goes to the gym all the time by the looks of his toned arms that the shirt is clinging to. I'm telling myself it's the alcohol controlling my thoughts even though the liquor has already started wearing off.

"Well, if you're not going to sleep in my room, then I am. Bathroom is down the hall, first door on the right. Only door on the right. Do you want a shirt or something to sleep in?"

Yeah right, like I'm going to sleep in his clothes.

My stomach growls as I reply, "No, but I do want a sandwich. You got any food? If you're going to keep me captive, the least you can do is feed me."

He lifts his chin gesturing to the kitchen. I walk in the small room pulling open the fridge to see pure heartbreak. Other than a stalk of celery that looks like the Jolly Green Giant's shriveled dick, a box of baking soda, and a carton of eggs, the fridge is empty. I let my shoulders sag as I shut the fridge. What I wouldn't give for some takeout right now.

He must sense my disappointment because he calls out from the living room, "There's some pasta in the cabinets. I'm sure there's stuff in there to make a peanut butter sandwich. There might be a pizza in the freezer. Eat whatever you want. I'm going to shower and go to bed."

I grab the loaf of bread and jar of peanut butter in the cabinet before rummaging through the drawers for a knife.

Asher disappears down the hall and returns with a blanket and pillow that he tosses on the couch.

"Don't worry; they're clean. I've only jerked off in the shower at this place," he says with a wink before disappearing down the hall again. I plop down on the couch with my peanut butter sandwich and hear the shower turn on.

I really fucked up coming back here.

Chapter 13

Tatum

I open my eyes to darkness. Sitting up, it takes a few minutes for my eyes to adjust. Fumbling for my phone, I groan from the pounding in my head. Clearly that pitiful peanut butter sandwich did nothing to ease my impending hangover. I tap the screen several times, but it doesn't light up. Fucking great, my phone is dead.

I stumble to the window by the front door. It's clearly still early because it's still dark outside other than the one lonely street lamp illuminating the parking lot. The snow is still falling in heavy blankets, and Asher's car is now completely white.

"This shit better be gone by morning," I mumble to myself. Rubbing my temples, I make my way to the bathroom in the hall. Surely there's some ibuprofen or something to ease my raging headache. Damn you, fruity alcohol.

I look in the mirror and about fall over. I look like shit. My makeup is completely smudged around my puffy eyes. My hair is a completely tangled mess, and my dress is covered in wrinkles. I use the bathroom and wash my face with some cold water before throwing my hair up in a messy bun. Thankfully I open the medicine cabinet and find some pain reliever and wash down two pills.

At this point I'm really starting to regret not taking Asher up on his offer to wear some of his clothes. This dress is too tight for comfort when I'm trying to sleep. Peeking my head around the bathroom door, I see two other rooms down the hall. One is closed and the other is just barely cracked open enough to let a sliver of moonlight shine into the hallway.

He offered me something to sleep in earlier so he shouldn't care now. Plus it's late enough that I'm sure he's asleep and I can just sneak in to grab a shirt without waking him. He shouldn't have offered if he'd get mad about it.

Making my way down to the first door which is closed, I gently push it open. It's almost completely empty save some boxes piled against the far wall. That leaves one other room. Asher's room.

Making my way to the room at the end of the hall, I push the cracked door open just enough to get a clear view inside. The room is illuminated by the moonlight spilling in through the windows. Soft snores from the bed tell me he is asleep. I can't see his face because he has the comforter up over most of his head, along with the rest of him. I can just see the top of his dark hair peeking out on his white pillow, and his foot is dangling over the side of the bed.

There's just enough moonlight streaming in the window to illuminate the room slightly. I see a dresser against the wall across from the bed, so I tiptoe as quietly as possible to the drawers. I don't have my phone to use as a flashlight, and the moonlight isn't enough to see well in the dark drawers. I reach in the second drawer assuming the first is socks and underwear. I rummage around with my fingers only feeling what I think is denim. Moving down to the next drawer, I feel around until I feel cotton on my fingertips and pull it out, clutching it to my chest as I quietly shut the drawer.

I freeze when I start to hear movement in the bed behind me. Without thinking, I dart out of the room, pressing myself flush against the wall just outside the door, heart racing. I don't know why I'm hiding like I'm guilty. I wasn't doing anything wrong, but part of me doesn't want to deal with him if he did wake up. Having a conversation with him is the last thing I want to do in my current hungover state.

Instead of making my way back to the bathroom to change, something tells me to peek around the corner to see if he woke up. But when I peek my head around the corner, my jaw drops to the floor and I throw my hand over my mouth to muffle the audible gasp that leaves me.

When I came in the room initially, Asher was almost completely covered with the blanket. Now he is not. The noises I heard must have been him shifting on the bed because he is now facing away from the doorway with the comforter kicked off most of his body. His naked body.

I know I shouldn't be looking, but I can't tear my eyes off of him. His chiseled arms and toned back muscles that were completely covered by his attire at the party. My eyes travel from his broad shoulders down to where the blanket stops right at his pelvis, hanging slightly off his hip. I know it's wrong, but I find myself wishing I could see the front view that I can tell isn't covered with the comforter. Allowing my gaze to go back to his arms, I can just barely make out the ink covering one of them which had been hidden by his long sleeve he wore to the party. It's too dark to tell what any of them are but I can tell two things. For one, it looks like a single detailed piece of artwork traveling from his shoulder down to his wrist. Secondly, I like it. I drag my lip across my bottom lip admiring my view.

Suddenly something shakes me out of the situation I'm in. What the fuck am I doing? I don't like this man. The man I'm looking at is a stranger, not the boy I knew eight years ago. In fact, I know nothing about the man laying in the bed in front of me.

I have a fiancé waiting for me back home. Why the fuck am I still standing here gawking at the body of a man who isn't my fiancé? I'm going to hell. I head back to the bathroom and pull on the t-shirt I yanked from his dresser and stare at myself in the mirror. I sigh when the smell of him wafts through my nose. Why do I feel like I don't even recognize the girl staring back at me? Clearly the alcohol is still in my system. That's why I'm acting like a complete idiot.

Making my way back to the couch, I slump down with a sigh realizing I'm anything but tired. I close my eyes and will myself to fall asleep, but instead my mind is reeling with mental images of what I saw in that bedroom and what I wish I had seen under that comforter. I let the images take over my brain until I drift to sleep.

✝

I wake up to the sun shining on my face and a sizzling sound coming from the kitchen. Rubbing my eyes and tossing the blanket off, I lift my bruised and aching ass off the couch and let my vision come into focus and see Asher standing over the stove.

"What time is it?" I ask as I stretch the ache out of my back from sleeping on the shitty couch all night.

"7:30," he says without looking up from whatever he's cooking. I make my way over to the window and look outside, the view making my heart sink.

"Shit."

"Yeah, the snow didn't let up like it was supposed to," I hear him say over my shoulder as I take in the solid white blanket covering everything outside. "I don't think the roads are going to be cleared any time soon."

"Well, I can't stay here. I need to get home. I'm only home, I mean *here* in Michigan until tomorrow night and Dad has been begging me for this visit so he's going to be pissed I'm missing this time with him."

I can't help but pace back and forth as anxiety and guilt takes over. My dad is going to be so upset. Not that I can control the weather, but I did choose going to Ari's party over staying in with him.

Asher must sense I'm getting tense because he looks over at me and says, "We'll get you home, but you need to eat something first. You have to be hungover from all that shit you drank last night."

I can hear the slight chuckle in his words which just fuels my anger about the entire situation.

"I took some ibuprofen last night, and actually what I *need* is a damn tooth brush. My mouth tastes like shit."

"I'm not surprised, mouth breather."

I can't help but gape at his words.

"I am not a mouth breather!"

I bring my hand up to cover my mouth hoping he's lying and that I did not lay on the couch with my mouth wide open while he stood over me watching me snore.

"Mmm hmm. You keep telling yourself that, Ms. Morning Breath. Don't worry, it's cute."

It's taking everything in me not to chuck something at his smiling face. His stupidly handsome smiling face, slight stubble covering his chin.

"Fuck off," I shout over my shoulder as I turn back to the window.

"There are some extra toothbrushes under the sink in my bathroom. You can use one."

Refusing to look at him, I make my way down to the bathroom. He must hear me turn on the light because I hear him yell from the kitchen, "Not that one! The bathroom in my bedroom. And don't even think about putting my toothbrush in the fucking toilet!"

I bark out a laugh because the thought hadn't crossed my mind until he suggested it, and now I totally am thinking about sticking his toothbrush in the toilet.

I head to his room and notice his bed is freshly made. Color me surprised that this man makes his bed in the mornings like an adult. I grab a toothbrush from under the sink and brush my teeth refusing to think about the fact that he probably keeps spare toothbrushes for his morning-after women he brings here.

I also fight the urge to rummage through his other bathroom cabinets. You can tell a lot about someone by what you find in cabinets and drawers. I don't look at myself in the mirror because I don't want to see how disheveled I know I look. Making my way back into his room, my mind flashes with images of his body in the moonlight. The image brings about feelings I don't want to feel so I shake the image from my head and approach the smell of food wafting down the hall.

When I turn the corner into the kitchen I stop as Asher's gaze rakes down my body causing goosebumps to erupt all over my skin. And then I remember I'm in his shirt. His shirt that is falling off of one shoulder and just barely covering my ass. When his eyes shoot back up to meet mine I stumble back a few steps feeling the blush creep across my cheeks and chest. Taking in the look in his eyes, I can't tell if his gaze is warm or angry.

"Uh, I'm gonna go get dressed," I say, pointing over my shoulder.

"Yeah," is all he says as I grab by dress from the night before off the floor and lock myself in the bathroom utterly mortified.

What the fuck is my life? I pull on my dress, missing the comfort that his shirt offered and head back to the living room where Asher is sitting with two plates on the coffee table.

"I hope scrambled eggs are good with you because it's all I've got for breakfast," he says, not even bothering to look up at me as I plop down on the cushion next to him.

"Scrambled eggs are fine. But then you're taking me home."

"Whatever you say, princess."

The condescending term makes me cringe and I shoot him a glare as I grab my fork and stab some eggs.

"How did you sleep?" he asks.

"Not great, but better than you'd expect on this shitty couch of yours."

"I offered you the bed, princess. You should've taken me up on my offer."

"Stop calling me that," I shoot at him, shoveling a bite of eggs into my mouth.

We finish the rest of our food in silence. Grabbing both empty plates from the coffee table I get up to take them to the sink. Halfway to the kitchen Asher speaks from the couch.

"You know, I almost thought you were going to crawl into bed with me last night with how long you stared at me from the doorway."

I freeze, suddenly feeling like the eggs I just ate are going to make their appearance again. I don't know how to talk myself out of this one so I continue walking to the sink.

Fuck. I thought he was asleep. How did he know I was watching him? He wasn't even facing me.

"I don't know what you're talking about."

"You got my shirt from somewhere. Was it not from my dresser?"

I can hear him making his way into the kitchen so I spin around to face him. "Well, yeah," I say defensively. "You said I could have some of your clothes and my dress got uncomfortable so I snuck in to grab a shirt. That's it. I was in and out, no staring involved."

"Hmm. Interesting. Your reflection in my window showed different."

Shit. The stupid window. I was so focused on wondering what his dick looked like that I didn't even think about the window. My silence clearly gave him the answer he was looking for because he's staring at me with a smirk that I have every urge to slap off his face. His ego is big enough without thinking I enjoy looking at his body. Which I don't just to be clear.

"Well, you must have been dreaming because I was not staring at you," I say, grabbing my phone from the couch to check the time but am greeted with a black screen.

"Shit. Can I borrow your phone charger?"

He disappears down the hallway and returns with a charger in hand giving it to me.

"Thanks," I mumble as I plug it into the wall and wait for the screen to turn on.

"Shit," I hiss as I look at the screen.

"Everything okay?" he asks.

"Uh, yeah, it's fine. Cayson called me like four times this morning." That's going to be lovely to explain why I couldn't answer him.

"Is Cayson the fiancé?"

My gaze shoots to his as he waits for an answer.

"Yes, he's the fiancé."

"How'd you meet him?" he asks.

"He was in one of my classes senior year of college."

"What's he do?" he asks as I continue to scroll through the notifications on my phone.

"He manages hedge funds."

"Hmm. Sounds fun."

I don't miss the smart ass tone in his voice so I shoot him a glare.

"Actually, it's good money and he enjoys it," I say, suddenly angry with his insinuation that it's a stupid job.

"Right. And what do you do?"

"Jesus, is this an interview?" I say. "I work from home part time while I'm finishing my master's degree."

"Master's huh? Impressive. I'm glad you didn't give up on your dream. What do you do for work? Trim hedge funds?"

Tossing my phone down on the cushions, I cross my arms and look at him.

"What's with the third degree?" I can tell he likes that he's getting a reaction from me which just pisses me off more since I'm giving him what he wants.

"I'm just asking questions."

"Too many of them."

"Come on. It's been eight years since I've seen you. You don't think it's fair for me to be curious about your life?" he asks as if we are casual friends just catching up.

"No."

"So you're not curious about mine?"

"Nope," I shoot at him, popping the p as I fall down on the couch cushions and realize my hangover is only getting enhanced by his annoying interrogation.

I notice my anxious habit of picking at my nails is ruining my manicure so I reach for a pencil wanting something to fidget with. I tense when I lean back and look at the pencil noticing the broken lead. I grab another pencil and freeze. Broken. I grab the last one. Broken. What the fuck? If I didn't know better I'd be convinced that he broke them on purpose before bringing me here. Tossing them all back on the table I throw myself back on the couch and notice Asher holding back a laugh.

"What?" I snap.

"Nothing," he says as he throws his hands up in the air.

Cayson's name lights up my phone screen and Asher's eyes linger on my phone like he's waiting to see if I answer it.

"I gotta take this," I say as I grab my phone and lock myself in the spare room down the hall away from listening ears.

"Hey, babe," I say into the phone, bracing for the impending argument that I've earned.

"Why haven't you answered any of my calls?"

I can tell there's anger laced in his words. I have no right to be upset that he's mad at me, but for some reason I am.

"I'm sorry. My phone died and I didn't have a charger so I didn't plug it in before I fell asleep."

"What were you doing?"

Is every man in my life just going to assault me with a bunch of questions?

"What do you mean?" I snap, suddenly feeling on edge. "I told you I went to a friend's party."

"Don't be pissy with me when you're the one not answering my calls."

His argumentative tone throws me off. He's been upset with me before, but not like this.

"Why are you so mad? You didn't talk to me all night because you were out with friends and somehow I'm in the wrong because my phone was dead?"

121

My hands are balled in fists at my side as I try not to lose it over the phone. My hangover isn't helping my attitude but his judgement is pissing me off. I purposely keep out the detail that I slept on my ex-boyfriend's couch knowing that would escalate the situation even further. Nothing happened so there's no reason for him to know.

"Well, considering I called your dad and he said you weren't at home, it's kind of strange, don't you think?"

"You called my dad? Why the fuck would you call my dad? How do you have my dad's number?"

I hear him huffing on the other end of the phone.

"Well, Tatum," he says with venom in his voice. "When your fiancée was out all night and you can't get ahold of her all morning, it makes you worry. So I called him and found it rather interesting that he said you didn't come home last night."

"I stayed with my friend! Not that it's any of your business. You were out with friends, too."

Except it totally is his business, but that's not what I'm feeling at the moment.

"Your *friend,* I'm sure."

I know exactly what he's insinuating and it just fuels my anger even though I know he has no idea who Asher is.

"I didn't do a damn thing wrong, Cayson. If you're insinuating what I think you are then you can call me back when you get your fucking attitude in check and stop judging a situation you know nothing about."

I hang up the phone and pace the room trying to collect myself. His usual calm demeanor was nonexistent and I don't know how to feel about it. My guilt is causing me to act out, and I know he has a right to be angry.

I'm not innocent in this situation, but I'm not as guilty as he's painting me to be either.

Going to Cayson's name I hit send and call him back figuring he won't answer. I'm surprised when the line connects, though he says nothing.

"I'm sorry I scared you, Cayson," I demure. Then I say all in one breath, "I'll be home in a few days. I'm just trying to enjoy this time with my dad and brother. The weather prevented me from getting home, so I stayed at my friend's. I'm going back as soon as the snow is clear. I just need a breather before the wedding. You know how stressful it's been between the wedding planning, my mom, school, and work. It's a lot to balance, and I just need a minute to myself."

I rub my thumb along my aching temple listening to his breath. Hearing nothing from him in response I say, "We're ok. I'll be home soon."

I think my last words were more about trying to assure myself than *him*. I hang up the phone and make my way back to the living room hoping Asher didn't hear the conversation that just ensued. I find him at the sink washing our dirty dishes from breakfast.

"Everything okay?" he asks over his shoulder as I enter the room.

"Yeah, it's fine," I say, even though I know it's not. That wasn't the end of the conversation with Cayson, but I don't feel like thinking about it.

"Anyway, I texted my dad. He's on his way to pick me up. So thanks for letting me stay."

I see his shoulders tense just slightly as he says, "Yeah, no problem. I'm gonna go wash up."

He exits the room and I hear his bedroom door shut.

I head to the bathroom and take in my appearance. The bags under my eyes are pronounced showing how well I slept last night. I shake out my hair and rake my fingers through the tangles the best I can and braid it messily over one shoulder. I decide I'll wait for my dad in the living room when I hear the shower in Asher's room turn on. I grab my phone and pull up my ebook. I forgot I left off on a steamy sex scene. The pages have me blushing, and as the main character grabs an ice cube from his glass on the table, I remember about my column that's due on Tuesday that I haven't even started. I remember now why I left off on the sex scene because I wanted some inspiration for my writing. I hear Asher's footsteps padding down the hallway, but before I can acknowledge his presence my phone rings and I slide my finger across the screen before putting it to my ear.

"Hey, Dad. Are you outside?"

"No, honey," he says. "I'm sorry, but I can't get to you."

"What? No, you said you were coming to get me!" I say, anxiety bubbling in my chest.

"My truck can't handle the weather. It's still having issues, and I only made it a couple miles down the road before I had to turn around. I'll have to wait until the plows clear the roads and have your brother come get you. He's closer to you than I am. The roads out in the country are just too bad."

"Why can't he just come get me now?" I can't help the frustration in my voice.

"You and I both know he's not a good driver in the snow, and I haven't been able to get ahold of him yet."

"No, Dad you have to come get me."

"I'm sorry, sweetheart. You know I want you here just as bad as you do. I promise I'll send your brother to come get you as soon as the roads are safe."

I don't sense much disappointment in his voice which makes me paranoid that he doesn't mind my absence. I know I'm just getting in my head and going crazy. Nothing about this weekend is going how it was supposed to.

"The roads should be cleared by tonight, and then we'll have most of the day tomorrow before your flight. It'll be okay."

I can't hold back the hurt and frustration in my voice as I say, "I didn't fly all the way home to spend one day with you dad."

"I know, sweetheart," he sighs. "I'm sorry. I'll let you know when the roads are clear."

With that he hangs up the call.

"Shit. Shit. Shit!"

"It's not a problem for you to stay here if that's what you're worried about."

I don't turn around as I wipe the tears from my eyes.

"It's not."

"Then what is it?"

"Nothing!" I snap, losing my patience from all of his questions.

I turn around ready to hurl my words at him until I take in his appearance. His dark curls are messy and damp on top of his head. He's not wearing a shirt, exposing the sleeve of tattoos I couldn't make out last night. Getting a better look in the daylight I can see how beautiful it is, all black and gray. A camera with film wrapping around his arm and melting into the rough waves of the ocean. There are birds flying above in the cloudy sky, and it suits him so well. His gray sweatpants hang low on his hips giving me a clear view of the V that leads to what I couldn't see last night. His abs are chiseled and there's a faint trail of dark hair disappearing into his sweats that are tight enough that they leave little to the imagination about what's underneath. When my eyes make their way back up to his face, I see the smirk on his face as he leans against the doorframe. Why does he have to look so good when he does that? It's like he doesn't even realize he's doing it.

Snapping myself out of my hypnotism, I plaster the best look of disgust I can on my face.

"Where's your shirt?"

"I didn't think I needed one," he says as if my question is an inconvenience. "I don't like wearing one around the house. I like to shower a lot. Saves me time to just take off my pants."

I cross my hands over my chest and huff at him.

"Well, you need one."

"Why? You didn't mind looking at me shirtless last night."

His accusation just pushes me further.

"For the last time, I was not staring at you! Get over yourself."

I can tell by the look on his face that he knows I'm full of shit. I am, but I will not admit that to him, or myself for that matter. I shouldn't have been looking at him anyway. It was a moment of weakness in a hungover state.

"Okay, so it's fine for you to walk around in my t-shirt and a skimpy little thong, but I can't walk around my own apartment without a shirt on?"

My heart pounds as I search for words. Then I find them: "I was uncomfortable in my dress, and I meant to wake up before you this morning so I could change but my phone died so my alarm never went off."

I never set an alarm. Why do I keep lying? I'm just digging myself into a deeper hole. I was in a state of shock seeing him practically naked which is why I didn't move. I wasn't ogling him. *I totally was.*

He stalks closer to me making me step back until he has me caged against the wall. My heart is pounding so hard I'm convinced he can hear my pulse. My tongue darts out to wet my lips as I stare up at him through my lashes. Why does he have to be so fucking attractive? I should be pushing him away and finding a way home, but I can't get my voice to work. I can't get my body to push him away; instead it's aching for him to get closer. He brushes a stray lock of my hair out of my face tucking it behind my ear leaning in, our lips a breath apart.

"I believe that about as much as I believe the lie about not staring at me naked in my bed," he whispers, his breath tickling my ear.

"You know what I think?" he asks. Without giving me a chance to answer, he keeps going: "I think you liked what you saw. I think you thought about what else was hiding under the covers and secretly you wanted me to find you in my shirt this morning. Deep down you wanted me to see my shirt hanging just low enough to cover the curve of your ass, leaving little to the imagination. How would it make you feel if I told you the sight of you staring at me had my dick growing so hard, I had to fight not to release my pain right in front of you? Fight the urge to pull your ass into my bed and fuck you until you forgot you hate me?"

I don't answer, and he keeps me trapped in his gaze and I can feel his growing erection against my thigh as he pushes in closer, urging my thighs apart with his knee.

"You wanted my eyes to linger," he continues. "You were hoping that my eyes would guide over your delicious body noticing your nipples poking through the shirt because you hadn't worn a bra under that tight ass dress last night. I should spank your ass raw for wearing that out for other people to see. You aren't happy with your man back in the place you call home and the thought of being with him for the rest of your life, having boring vanilla sex for all the years to come makes you want to gag so you came here hoping for an escape."

He brushes my braid off my shoulder and plants the lightest kiss on my collarbone causing goosebumps to erupt all over my skin.

"Then you saw me and you wanted to keep hating me but you couldn't. You couldn't fight the urge to look at me and wonder what you've been missing, what life would've been like with me if you would've stayed. That's why you let me put you in my car and that's why you let me bring you here, and that's why you snuck into my room last night, not leaving when you saw my body."

The breath is leaving my lungs like I'm being deflated. The look in his sparkling green eyes is about to make my knees buckle. His lips are so close to mine that I can't help but wonder what they would feel like if he captured mine in a kiss, ravaging my mouth like a savage. My body unwillingly lets out a whimper and he hears it. By the jerk of his erection and the smile on his face, he liked it.

"You'd love if I picked you up and took you to my bed. Hell, I bet you'd let me take you right here on the floor. You wouldn't fight it if I ripped this dress off of you and kissed every inch of your skin, teasing your clit until you were begging for release. You'd let me sink my dick so deep inside you over and over until you couldn't walk tomorrow. You'd cry out my name as I fucked you in every room of this apartment and you'd squirm, wanting more until I made you come. On my tongue. On my fingers. On my cock. And that's why I can guarantee that if I reached under that dress right now, I'd feel how soaking fucking wet you are. That's what I think.

Color me speechless, because what the fuck? He pushes off the wall distancing himself from me, and I find my body aching to feel him close again, feel the warmth of his touch on my skin. I want to feel his minty breath against my face. I want to watch his eyes flash to my lips when I wet them with my tongue. I can feel the blush covering my skin, and by the gleam in his eyes, he's noticed it too. Fucking asshole. He takes pleasure in this.

Suddenly the anger rages through me. He wanted a reaction from me, and I played into his stupid game like a child. I was stupid enough to think he actually wants me. Snatching my phone from the coffee table I storm into the bathroom and lock the door.

"You are absolutely the asshole I thought you were!" I scream through the door. He doesn't get to win this manipulative game.

"Hide all you want, princess, but we both know I'm right."

I can hear the smile in his words and I want to slap it off his face. He is fucking right, and I hate that he is.

"Like it or not, you're stuck until the roads are clear so you might as well accept it."

I put my back to the door and let myself drop to the floor, head in my hands. Why do I feel so flustered? I'm letting him get exactly what he wants from me, messing with my head. I don't have feelings for this man. It's been eight years. He lied to me, deceived me. I lied to *him* and deceived *him*. I'm getting married, and this is wrong. All wrong.

So why does it feel so good to think about the way he made my body feel in the living room minutes ago? And why do I want it to happen again? I pound my head against the door trying to clear my brain of my thoughts concerning Asher. He's not the one who is supposed to be consuming my thoughts, sending shivers through my body, making me ache with need.

"When is the wedding anyway?" he asks from the other side of the door.

I hesitate before answering.

"Three weeks from today."

"Are you happy?"

I can tell by his tone that he's asking with sincerity. He truly wants to know. So I do the best thing I can think of. I don't answer him. I start the shower, hoping he takes my silence as his cue to leave me alone, and hoping that the hot water will wash these feelings out of my body. I love Cayson. I'm getting married to Cayson. My future is with Cayson. We are going to have the happy ending my mother always–I always dreamed of. But I can't fight the sinking pit I feel in my stomach when I think about the wedding that is rapidly approaching, and the vows I haven't written.

I don't want Asher. I *can't* want him. I ran away eight years ago for something he can never know about. I gave him the freedom we both needed, the freedom he deserved. We weren't meant to end up together.

I finally hear him stand up and walk away from the door. Huffing out a sigh of relief that he let the conversation go, I check my phone. Ari sent me a text asking if I got home safe last night. I feel bad for not telling her goodbye, but I was in no condition.

I shoot off a quick text letting her know Asher brought me back to his apartment until the roads clear and ask how she's feeling this morning because I know she had a hefty dose of liquor, too. All I get in response is *My brother's, huh?* with a winky face. Whatever that's supposed to mean.

I hop in the shower letting the hot water rinse away my shame.

Chapter 14
Asher

I'm sitting on the couch watching something stupid and mindless on the TV when I hear the bathroom door crack open. A few minutes later I don't spare her a glance as she makes her way into the living room.

"Are you done pouting?"

"I wasn't pouting," she lies. "Okay, princess?"

I can't help but chuckle at her attempt to insult me with the term I've been using on her.

I feel her plop down on the couch next to me and ignore the way my body responds to her presence, the smell of my body wash on her skin. I hate that I love being close to her, and I hate that everything I accused her of earlier had me fighting not to jerk off to the idea of it as soon as she got in the shower, or busting through the bathroom door and showering with her.

"What do you do?" She reads my expression and clarifies: "For work. What do you do for work? Are you still doing photography?"

I allow myself to admire her face for a second before I return my gaze to the TV. Her wet hair is pulled up in a bun with a few pieces framing her face. I didn't think it was possible for her to be more beautiful than she was eight years ago. My memory did not do her justice. Fuck me. My eyes drink her in when I realize she's wearing another one of my shirts. She must have grabbed it after her shower. This one is bigger than the last so it falls lower on her short frame, about mid thigh. It should not look that good on her, but of course it fucking does, and of course the sight of it has my neglected dick stirring again. She's even more stunning than I remember, and I have to force my eyes away from her when she licks her lips again.

"Oh. No. I work for a law firm in San Diego," I tell her.

She looks at me with a face of shock and *disappointment?*

"Wow," she says. "That's a big jump from photography. I thought you wanted to travel? What happened to the magazine gig?"

"I did. I mean I do," I stutter. Explaining this should not be that difficult. "I worked for the magazine for a year, but it wasn't as successful as we'd hoped and I needed something more…" I don't want to say it, "stable. I started school and got a paid internship with a law firm as an administrative assistant. They helped me fast track my undergrad degree, and I've been there since. I'm still working on my degree for law school, but I'll be done next semester, then all I have to do is pass the Bar exam."

I spare her a glance and hate myself for it when I see the interest in her eyes.

"It's a small firm," I admit, "and they say I show a lot of promise so they've already promised me a position as an attorney once I pass the Bar. It's not what I imagined for myself, but it's a stable career, good money, and law is actually more interesting than I thought it would be."

I leave out the part that I actually hate the job because I don't want her to know how miserable my life has been since she left. The job that ended our relationship was laughable and now I'm going to school for something I don't like just so I have security. Meanwhile she's engaged, getting her master's, and has a steady job. She's thriving.

She adjusts herself on the couch, pulling her thighs up to her chest. But when I look down, I about bust in my pants. She's not wearing any underwear. I figured she had a pair of my boxers on or something. I cannot pry my eyes off of her pussy. And suddenly I can't help but imagine how good it would feel to bury myself deep inside of her.

She must realize what she did because she's moving to the far side of the couch and pulling the shirt down as far as she can, the blush rapidly covering her chest and face. Her eyes dart to me when she sees the erection in my sweats. What the fuck did she expect? This woman is going to be the death of me. Every second I'm around her I'm holding myself back from fucking her.

I could push her about the fact that she seems to be affected by me too, but I'm going to save that ammunition for later. I don't bother to fix the erection straining my sweats because there's no hiding it. She's not explaining herself or trying to dig herself out of the situation at all though she's clearly embarrassed. Interesting.

I clear my throat and turn back to the TV trying to remember what the fuck I was talking about before she flashed me that delectable pussy. It takes me a minute to regather my thoughts.

"That's why I, um, don't get to see Mom, Dad, and, um…" *don't forget your sister's name, idiot*, "Ari as often as I'd like because I have so much on my plate between the, um, office and school. I wasn't sure I'd be able to get time off to come to the party so I didn't get her hopes up. Granted, I don't know why she's getting married but I know she wanted me there."

"Do you not like Liam?"

Liam, right. She's in town one day and she knows Ari's fiancé's name. She's clearly nicer than I am.

"No, it's not that," I tell her. "I have nothing against the guy. We've hung around each other a few times. I just want the best for her, and I think she's too young to be deciding who she wants to be with forever."

She focuses her gaze on something across the room.

"I see you still hate the idea of marriage."

That was always such a sensitive topic for her, and by the way she's tensing up, it apparently still is.

"I never *hated* the idea," I say, recalling our breakup over this same fucking subject. "I just didn't think it was for me."

The word 'didn't' snaps her gaze towards me, so I clarify: "I don't know that it will ever be for me... anymore."

I look at her and can't make out the look in her eyes. Hurt? Guilt? She doesn't say anything, so I continue: "With what I wanted to do in life it just didn't make sense. Marriage maybe, but I don't think you need a piece of paper telling you that you love each other to stay together. Back in high school I knew I loved you and I wanted to be with you, but marriage was so distant in my mind. I just wanted to be with you while doing what I wanted with my life. And the idea of kids just didn't seem fair. The plan was to travel, and then I got the internship and I was supposed to be all over the place for work. I wouldn't want a dad that made me move all the time for his job so why would I do that to my own child?"

The honest words are starting to make me feel guilty for treating her like shit about something she did as a teenager. I did love her, and I think I still do as I look at her and remember how she made me feel. She was the constant in my life that kept me grounded, and if I ever pictured a future with anyone, it would be her–*would've* been her.

She's staring at the floor spinning her ring around her finger, and it feels like a knife is twisting into my gut as I think about the fact that she's marrying another man. About the fact that another man gets to make love to her in his bed.

The last time we had this conversation, she got so mad and wanted to have the last word, but now she's so quiet and calm that I just keep talking: "I wanted to travel and take pictures of what I saw in the process. I still love photography and I think it will always be a part of me. I didn't want a family to hold me back or vice versa. After you left, or I guess after I got to California and could only afford Ramen, I started to realize I wanted more for myself. I wanted more stability so *if* I ever did change my mind in the future about having a family, I could have it."

My mind starts racing with images of a marriage with her, of the life she threw away because I let her. With her swollen stomach as she carries my baby. The image of waking up to her in my sheets every morning. Her words shake me out of my mind.

"Have you?" she asks with a tone that sounds broken, her eyes locked on mine. "Changed your mind, I mean?" Like the wrong answer will shatter her to pieces.

"I don't know," I say honestly after a couple of seconds. "Sometimes I like the idea of having a mini me running around the big house I plan to buy when I become an attorney...IF I become an attorney. Then other times I think about the fact that I'm practically still a kid myself and I don't know how I'd be capable of taking care of a tiny human. I don't feel like I'd be good at the whole dad thing."

She's looking at me and hanging on my every word. Any sense of hatred has melted from her eyes as she stares back at me with those gorgeous eyes I love staring into, used to love staring into.

"Despite how terrible you think I am," I say, wanting to reach out and take her hand, "I wouldn't want my wife taking care of everything for my child on her own."

Tate's face pales and her features tighten. It's quick and then it's gone like she buried whatever she was thinking deep within. I wouldn't have noticed if I hadn't been focused on her beautiful brown eyes as she watched me.

She clears her throat before reaching for the remote and flipping through the channels. I know what she's going to pick before she even lands on it. A stupid crime show with an unrealistic plot with "cops" that are far too attractive to actually be cops. I take this as a hint that our eight-year-old conversation is over... again... for now.

"I'm getting hungry," I ask, trying to relieve whatever tension has clouded the air. "Are you?"

"Even if I said yes, what would we eat? There's practically nothing in your kitchen and ordering something is out of the question," she says, gesturing outside at the window, and I can't help but chuckle at the irritation in her voice. She's always had a habit of getting hangry.

"Don't worry about that. I don't need food in the kitchen," I assure her. "What do you like? Are you still as picky as you were back then?"

I remember how awful it was to feed this woman in high school. She refused to eat anything that wasn't mashed potatoes, pasta, or pizza.

"No," she says, clearly lying.

"Is baked spaghetti still your favorite?"

Her face widens with a smile like she's incredibly happy I remembered. She made it impossible to forget almost anything about her, ingraining my memories with her into my brain like they're a part of my DNA. Like my mom cooking her mac and cheese because she wouldn't eat tacos on taco Tuesday.

"Pretty much anything with pasta or cheese is my favorite."

"Shocking. I'll be right back."

I stand up and grab a shirt and shoes from my room before slipping out the door without giving her any indication of what I'm doing.

I walk down two doors and knock on the apartment door. Just like I expected, she's home, and she opens the door with a smile on her face as she does every time I stop by her doorstep. After a quick explanation she agrees without hesitation, refusing the twenty dollar bill I try to slip her. Typical.

When I walk back into my apartment, Tate is looking at me patiently waiting for an explanation.

"She'll have lunch ready in an hour," I say.

She looks at me puzzled.

"What do you mean *she'll* have lunch ready in an hour?" she asks. Then her face tightens. "Oh my god, you're sleeping with someone in the apartment complex aren't you? You're having your girlfriend cook lunch for you."

Her question sounding more like a statement.

"What the fuck, Asher? Why didn't you stay in her apartment last night?"

It's cute that she's jealous, and I'm not at all surprised by her irrational thoughts. She's fidgeting in her place on the couch and biting her lip the same way she used to when she got flustered. Will she fidget that shirt up just a little more again? Of course my dick takes notice of it too. I laugh at her accusation and sit back down on the couch, adjusting myself so she can't see my straining erection yet again. I'm going to have serious blue balls after this weekend.

"Do you remember Miss Borden?"

"Miss Borden? As in our ninth grade history teacher?"

"Yes. She lives two doors down. She moved in shortly after I did and it happened to be a weekend that I was home. I helped her move her stuff in and now she cooks for me sometimes when I'm here visiting."

I can tell by her face that she's embarrassed by her accusation that I was fucking someone else in the complex, and I don't plan on letting her forget about her jealousy, or admit that I find it sexy.

"She says a man my age doesn't know how to cook for himself," I smile. "She's not wrong. Her husband died a few years ago and she lost the house. She never had kids so she doesn't really have anyone else. I think I've become the son she never had."

I look at her hoping she sees the humor in my eyes. She seems to, so I say, "I asked her if she'd be willing to make a lunch for two. You should've seen the look on her face when I told her I needed two helpings instead of one. She'd probably croak if I told her it was for you. She talks about you every time I see her."

That confession clearly piques her interest as she perks up looking at me.

"Why does she talk about me?"

"She remembers you, and that we were best friends. She knows we were more than that at one point and she adored you. Little Miss straight A's couldn't have been a better student."

I roll my eyes playfully and she returns it, her lips turning up slightly at the corners. I can feel her thawing, starting to reciprocate some of my playful banter.

"She used to always ask if we were still close," I say, "but I didn't have the heart to tell her how we ended. She just thinks we lost contact over the years when you went to school, but she doesn't know any of the details about why."

I can tell she doesn't know how to respond, so she stays quiet.

We watch TV in silence for about an hour when there's a knock on the door. When I open it, Miss Borden is standing there with a wide smile on her face which only gets bigger when Tate walks up behind me placing herself into view.

I turn around and see she's covering herself in a blanket from the couch. No doubt she's trying to hide the fact that she's in nothing but my shirt. Miss Borden would have a heyday with that one. Though Tate's disheveled appearance from this weekend accompanied by the fact that she's hiding under a blanket probably isn't giving off the facade she thinks it is. And by the grin on Miss Borden's face, I think my assumption is correct.

"Here you are, dear," Miss Borden says. "Just throw it in the oven at three fifty for ten minutes to heat it up. I assume you can at least pre–heat the oven."

She chuckles and hands me two dishes.

"This is an apple crisp," she says. "It's left over from Thanksgiving, but I thought you two could use some dessert, too."

She winks at me and I suppress a laugh before taking the pans to the kitchen to pre-heat the oven. I hear her start to talk to Tatum as I leave the room so I pretend to busy myself in the kitchen so I can listen in on their conversation. Thankfully, the woman has lost her hearing with age and is talking well above a whisper.

"He still fancies you, ya know. He would never admit it, but he talks about you every time I see him," she tells Tate.

Shit. I wait, anticipating a response from Tate, but a bout of silence follows instead. It's killing me not to look in their direction to see her reaction.

"He harbored hard feelings after you left, but I don't think there's anything you could do to keep him from loving you. He's a good man, Tatum. Don't let him scare you off again; you're good for him."

Well, this can't happen. I walk out of the kitchen to put an end to their conversation.

"What are we talking about, ladies?" I say as I open the front door hinting for Miss Borden to leave. I'm avoiding Tate's stare that I feel digging into the side of my skull. I'm not surprised since this woman just told her something completely different from what I did an hour ago. I wasn't completely lying. Miss Borden does talk about her a lot, and she did adore Tate in school, but she does know how we ended. She has acted as my therapist, listening to my bitching more than I care to admit.

"Oh, nothing," Miss Borden lies. "Just telling Tatum how much I loved having her in class. You two were always such a hoot. Anyway, I'll leave you two to your food. I cooked enough to have leftovers for dinner if you need it. And don't worry about the dishes, honey. I've got plenty of those pans."

"Thank you, Nancy," I say. "Let me know if you need me to clean off your car in the morning before church."

I can feel eyes boring into my back as I shut the door. She knows I lied. If she asks, I'm not admitting shit. But when I turn around and see the look on her face, what feels like adoration, I suddenly feel like pushing buttons to get an admission out of her.

"What did she say to you?" I ask.

"Nothing worth sharing."

"Somehow I know that's a lie," I say, wanting to be pissed at her but finding I can't.

"I was just telling the cougar that I'll be gone by tonight so she can come stake her claim on her prey."

There's a sparkle in her eye as she chuckles at her own joke.

"Did you just call our old ninth grade teacher a cougar?"

"Oh, I'm sorry. I mean Nancy," she says in a singsong voice before biting her bottom lip between her teeth to hold back her laugh.

"We both know she's not my type," I say.

I stalk over to her bending down until I'm hovering inches from her face, her scent intoxicating me as I whisper in her ear. "And the only prey in this room is right in front of me practically begging to get eaten."

She throws a hand over her mouth when she realizes she's audibly whimpered, crimson staining her cheeks from embarrassment. She should know by now not to poke the bear if she can't handle the response.

The oven beeps letting me know that it's pre-heated so I retreat to the kitchen and throw the pan of cheese covered pasta in, setting a timer for ten minutes and go back to the living room where Tate is scrolling through the channels on the TV, her thighs clenched as if she's uncomfortable.

"There's nothing worth watching on here," she huffs as she tosses the remote and slouches back like a child.

I snatch the remote and laugh when she proves my point and crosses her arms over her chest. I flip through until I settle on something and toss the remote on the table.

"A zombie show, really? You used to hate these and always said they were stupid. You always made fun of Jace for watching them."

"They are stupid," I say, "But now I appreciate them for their stupidity and humor. Besides, this one is good because the zombies actually move at a terrifying pace. If you can't outrun a dead cripple that moves two miles an hour, you deserve to die in the apocalypse."

I ignore her as she looks at me with a gaping mouth like I just told her I murdered an innocent puppy.

When the oven beeps, I go to the kitchen to grab our food and grab two glasses of water.

"Sorry, water is all I've got to drink unless you want some bourbon or a shot of tequila," I say, handing her the plate and glass with a knowing grin on my face.

"Water is fine. Thank you. We both know tequila and I don't get along."

I know. By the smile on her face I can tell she's remembering the same night I am. The sex was great, but I'm sure she mostly remembers puking her guts out the next morning while I held her hair. I grab my plate and glass from the kitchen before sitting next to her.

"So you and Ari are still close, I see," she says, taking a bite of her food.

"We talk almost every day when I get a free minute. She knows I can't get home as often as I'd like so we stay in touch as much as possible."

"Have you thought about moving back closer to home if you miss her so much? I'm sure there's another law firm somewhere closer that would take you on."

I have to keep myself from staring at her and resist the urge to lick the smudge of sauce from the corner of her mouth.

"I'd be lying if I said the thought hasn't crossed my mind. I'm still just an assistant at the firm so there's technically nothing keeping me from moving closer. I could transfer all of my classes online. Ari doesn't want to be the reason I move back though."

"Why? She's family. It makes sense that you'd want to be close to her and your parents."

I hesitate before answering her, suddenly feeling a lump in my throat that I can't swallow.

"She doesn't want to be the *only* reason I move back," I say.

She stops chewing, and for a second I think she's going to press me on what I mean, but she doesn't. But her reaction tells me she knows exactly what I meant. I hate that her presence is pulling so much honesty from my mouth.

"So what about you?" I ask, changing the conversation. "Do you ever think about moving back home? Once you get married?"

"To this small town where everyone makes it their business to know my business?" She snorts like it was a stupid question. "No. I can't say I don't miss Michigan overall; it has some perks, but I don't think I could live in this town again. Not to mention this weather sucks ass. I think I'm a warm weather girl through and through. Michigan doesn't feel like my home… anymore."

The look of hurt in her eyes is present for a second before it dissipates as she takes her last bite of food.

"Cayson wouldn't move though, even if I wanted to," she says, licking sauce from her lips. "All of his family is in Florida and he's kind of a momma's boy. Both with his mom and mine."

I can't contain my curiosity seeing as this is the most insight she's given me about the mystery man that gets to claim her as his.

"He wouldn't move even if that was what you wanted?" I ask.

This topic feels all too familiar, but it doesn't seem to bother her as she ponders the question.

"I don't think so," she says. "I mean, we've never had a serious conversation about it because I don't think I want to move, but he's always said he wants to stay in Florida. Plus my mom loves him. She'd have a conniption if I tried to take him from her. So would he."

I snort at her comment. This man sounds like an infant.

"Your mom likes him, huh? She always hated me."

143

That earns me a chuckle from her. She's so fucking adorable when she laughs.

"Yeah, she did. Well, after we started dating anyway. I don't think you were her favorite before that, but making it official really seemed to push her over the edge. You know how she is. She's always had my life planned out in her head, and you weren't in her plan. She didn't take that well."

I know I shouldn't, but I want to dig deeper into this conversation.

"Why? Because I wasn't the pretty rich boy she had in mind?"

She looks beautiful when she's in her thoughts. I can tell she's getting lost in her mind because she's picking at her nails and avoiding looking at me when she talks.

"Essentially," she admits. "You weren't the white picket fence type. I love my mom, but I won't deny that she's a lot to handle sometimes, especially now. Our relationship hasn't been the same since…"

She trails off and when she looks up I can see the tears starting to form in her eyes. Something clearly happened between them, and I hate that my heart hurts seeing her hurt. I fight the urge to wrap my arms around her and wipe the tears with the pads of my thumbs. I'm about to fish for information on what happened when she wipes the tears from her eyes and starts to talk, trying to avoid the topic.

"Lunch was delicious," she says, checking my t-shirt for anything she may have spilled. "You're lucky Miss Borden, I mean Nancy, likes you enough to cook for you. I'm dying to taste dessert."

Me too. But not the apple crisp she's referring to. I don't realize I've been staring at her mouth until she clears her throat which brings my gaze to hers.

I get up and grab her plate wanting to place as much space between us as possible because the feelings she's evoking from me are confusing the hell out of me.

"I'm going to get a glass of bourbon. You sure you don't want some?" I ask over my shoulder. My lips upturn slightly at the sound of her groaning in disgust. Dark liquor was never her thing.

"Yeah, I'm sure. Either Dad or Jace will be here in a couple of hours anyway."

No they won't, but she doesn't need to know that. This town has one snow plow, and they don't make it a priority to clear the country roads. Not that it would have mattered anyway, but who am I to smother her hope that she's getting out of this apartment any time soon? The idea of her being trapped here makes me happier than it should. I make my way back to the couch, bourbon in hand and her dessert in the other when I see her phone light up with that man child's name flashing on the screen. I'm expecting her to answer but she flips the phone over instead.

"You can take that," I say settling into the cushion next to her, noting the fact that she doesn't shift away when my leg brushes hers through the blanket draped over her lap.

"It's fine. I told him I'd call him later," she says as she scoots the tiniest bit closer, putting her thigh flush with mine. Troublemaker.

"You don't seem very thrilled when you talk about him."

I shouldn't be pushing it, but I can't help it with her.

"What? No, it's not that," she says. The tone of her voice is anything but convincing, but maybe I'm trying to convince myself that's the truth.

"I mean it's just the stress of everything. This wedding hasn't exactly been the most fun for me to plan like I wanted it to be. My mom pretty much took over everything."

I'm not surprised. That woman liked control, especially concerning Tate, but I don't vocalize that. Though from the vibe I got earlier, I don't think she'd disagree with me on it.

"Do you even want this wedding?" I ask honestly.

The question must catch her off guard because she shoots me a panicked look as she chokes on her bite of food, struggling to clear her throat as she gulps down the rest of her water.

"What do you mean by that?"

"The things your mom has planned. Is it even what you want for your wedding?" We both know that's not what I'm actually asking.

"Oh. I mean I don't really care. She's just making it a bigger deal than I would have. I thought I always wanted some big elaborate wedding, but all of this planning turning into exactly that has proven that I'm much simpler than I thought."

"My question made you choke on your food. Did you think I meant something different with my question? What was your interpretation?"

She ignores my question and stands up heading to the kitchen.

"On second thought, I will take that shot of tequila."

She only makes it a few feet before muttering under her breath, "God knows I have to be intoxicated in order to stand you."

Smart ass. Also not true considering she's been dealing with me all of today without any alcohol.

I follow her quietly into the kitchen watching her take the shot, containing my laugh when she cringes at the taste, causing her whole body to shiver. She's facing away from me, hands braced on the counter as I make my way closer.

"I thought you and tequila didn't get along. Didn't you always tell me tequila was your enemy?"

She doesn't turn around as she pours herself another generous shot and downs it. Gutsy considering how much she drank last night. At least she has food in her system this time.

"Yeah, well keep your friends close and your enemies closer, right?"

I know she can feel my presence as I get closer to her. I'm not close enough to touch her. *Yet.* But she knows I'm there even though she refuses to turn around. I have a feeling it's because she knows I'll see right through this facade of hers when she looks me in the eyes.

"So, what about you? You have a girlfriend?"

"Why? Would you be jealous if I did?" I say to the back of her head.

It's a genuine question even though there's humor in my tone. I want her to know I haven't had a girlfriend since her, but I don't say it. No woman would ever compare to her and I'd be stupid to think otherwise.

"You really are full of yourself, aren't you? Not every woman wants to fuck you."

She's playing into my game, and I love it. She's cute when she's flustered.

"No, I wouldn't be jealous. I'm getting married, remember?"

She throws up her left hand pointing to the obnoxiously large diamond ring on her finger over her head still making a point not to look at me. I take note of the fact that she obviously didn't have a say so in the ring choice.

"Yeah, you seem so keen on the man that you run away from him three weeks before the wedding."

That does the trick. She's whipping around to face me, anger clear on her face. That's right, look at me, beautiful. Angry or not, I love looking into her eyes, drowning in the golden brown flames that stare back at me.

"I didn't run away from him," she says, her tequila breath warming my face. "He knows I'm here."

"But yet you didn't bring him with you."

I'm slowly closing the space between us as she plasters herself against the counter trying to increase the distance. Good luck with that, princess.

"Tell me, Tate, are you happy with him?"

I give her time to remove herself from my presence if she wants to, leaving enough space for her to squeeze around me, but she's not moving. She's not running away from me. She ran away from him, but she's not running away from me. By the way her breathing is getting shallow, and the way she's biting her lip, she wants me close.

"Why do you care so much about my relationship?" she asks, trying to avoid eye contact. "It was pretty clear last night how you felt about me, so why are you acting like you care?"

There's no venom in her voice. She's curious, and that makes my dick hard as a fucking rock. For the fucking fiftieth time since I saw her last night.

Her voice cracks as she says, "I'm not the same Tatum you grew up with. I'm not the same girl you remember."

I don't answer and my silence seems to piss her off slightly.

"You don't know anything about me anymore," she spits, anger and pain in her voice as she tries to walk around me. "And it's obvious you still resent me for leaving so just leave me alone."

I grab her arm and twist her to face me, my lips inches from hers. The irritation radiating from her body has my dick straining painfully with the urge to fuck her raw right here in the kitchen. This fucking woman.

"You're right, Tate. After you left me all those years ago, I swore I would never feel anything but hatred for you. The girl I loved wouldn't have thrown us away like that. Couple or not, we were so much more than that. I held on to hope for a while after you disappeared, hoping you'd come back to me with an explanation." Her eyes soften as she watches me.

"Maybe you just needed space. But then that hope dissipated and turned into hatred. Every time I thought about you over the years I would get so angry because clearly you didn't love me like I loved you."

Using the word 'love' in past tense feels like acid on my tongue because I know I'm lying to both of us.

"But then I came back for my sister's party. When I walked in and saw you I tried so fucking hard to hold onto that anger. I should've gone the whole night without talking to you and went on about my life, keeping you as far away as possible. But I couldn't stop staring at you in that fucking dress."

She's holding on to every word that leaves my mouth and I can tell she's trying to convince herself that I mean it. Staring at her face, into her gorgeous fucking eyes, I'm so glad I didn't walk away when I saw her last night. Even if she shatters me again, being around her makes it worth it.

"And then you had to get drunk and try to walk home by yourself. I couldn't watch you walk home alone. And if we're being honest with ourselves, Tate, I don't think you hate me as much as you want me to believe you do. It's not even like you have a reason to hate me. You're the one that walked away." I pause, leaning down to rest my forehead against hers, relaxing when she doesn't pull away.

"I didn't tell you about the job, but I was going to once I figured out how to make it work. How to make *us* work through it all. So if you're using this fake hatred to cover up the fact that you still want me, that you are hoping I still feel the same about you, I don't think either of us have been very honest this weekend."

She's fighting to keep her composure. She wants to believe I'm toying with her. Fine, at first I probably was–okay, I was–but I'm done lying to myself, denying the fact that I want her. I'm going to crack her no matter how hard she fights me. This woman has been and always will be my fucking undoing. Just when I thought I was figuring it all out without her, her presence invaded my fucking mind, my life, and I'll be damned if I let her walk away again without admitting the truth to both of us.

"Well, I can see your vivid imagination hasn't changed over the years."

Her response is mediocre. Her resolve is falling apart and I can see it in her eyes as she darts them around the room. I push her back until she's pressed against the counter, caging her in between my arms as I palm the counter and push back the stray hair in her face as I lean in to whisper in her ear.

"You're right about that. I am imagining a *lot* of things right now, Tate."

I can see the fight in her eyes as her brain battles her body. Her tongue darts out to wet her lips, her thighs clenching as she swallows before looking at me with lustful eyes.

"Like what?" She asks just above a whisper. *Dirty girl.*

I can't help the smile plastering my face as I place my hands on either side of her body, lightly brushing my thumbs up her sides as I block her in. She could push me away if she wanted to, I'm not forcing this, and I wouldn't stop her if she tried to walk away because as bad as I'd want to, I know once I get a taste of her, I'm fucking done for. There will be no coming back.

"I can show you instead. All you have to do is ask."

I press my body to hers, pushing my erection into her stomach to show her how much I want her so there's no confusing the situation.

"I'm not asking, I'm telling you, Tate. Ask me to show you. I remember how much you always loved being told what to do."

"Like I said Ash, you don't know me anymore."

Oh but I fucking want to. I want to know everything about her, who's she's become, everything I've missed. She can't hide the desire in her eyes even as she looks away, thinking she hid it before pointing her gaze at the floor. She wants this to happen just as much as I do, she just can't win the battle going on in her mind. But I'm going to make her prove to me she wants me as much as I want her. Except I don't want her, I fucking *need* her. She's looking at everything but my face because she knows what will happen if she looks at me. I grab her chin and force her to look up at me, my eyes going straight to her mouth. God, those lips would look so fucking pretty wrapped around my cock.

"Tell me what's going through that pretty little head of yours."

"No."

She jerks her head out of my grasp looking down at the floor, but still leaving herself trapped in my presence.

"Bet you twenty bucks I can tell you exactly what you're thinking about, princess."

"No."

"Why? Because you know you'd lose? Because you know I'd be able to steal the words from your filthy mouth? I fucking love that by the way. Because you're thinking filthy things that you refuse to admit to yourself?"

Her lips press into a thin line as the anger resurfaces. Such a feisty thing she is.

"Fine. That's twenty bucks in my pocket since you don't know a damn thing."

She pushes against my chest moving around me going back to the living room.

"Well, go ahead then," she says. "What am I thinking?"

She whips around to face me, hands folded over her chest.

Challenge accepted. She asked for it and denied every chance I gave her to walk away from this.

"See, here's the thing, Tate…"

I walk closer to her until she's back up against the living room wall. I lean down and run my nose along her jawbone speaking just loud enough she can hear the words leaving my mouth.

"You're thinking about how you wish I'd fuck you right here. You're imagining what my lips will taste like when they take yours. You've got a mental picture in your head of what I look like on my knees as I push my shirt up your body, exposing that gorgeous wet pussy of yours that you aren't trying to hide since we both know you're not fucking wearing anything under this shirt. Trying to show me how wet I make you? You want to remember what it will feel like when I trace my tongue over your clit making you buck as you try to increase the pressure, riding my fingers as they fuck you."

Pulling the fabric of my shirt away from her thighs I rub it between my fingers noticing how she's squirming. She has to end this before I cross the line, because I can't fucking end it. My willpower is almost obsolete at this point.

"You're thinking about what is hiding underneath these sweats, and what you didn't get to see when you were spying on me last night. You're hoping you don't leave this apartment without knowing what my tongue feels like on your body, inside of you. What the veins in my cock feel like as they pulse in your mouth when you suck me off. You want to know what my cock feels like when it's buried so deep inside of you that you're screaming my name because you want to know if it feels better than you remember. And I know you fucking remember, because I remember how amazing your pussy felt, how fucking good it felt when you took my cock like the good girl you are."

She's whimpering, and I can tell in her eyes that she's barely hanging on. *Just let go.* I look down making sure she follows my gaze to her trembling legs.

"You're fidgeting because you're trying to distract yourself to ease the pain of the arousal that you can't deny. We both know that if I trailed my fingers up this shirt, I'd find you dripping wet, ready for me to fuck you." I dart my tongue out, lightly trailing up her throat as she throws her head back to give me better access.

"With my tongue."

Lick.

"With my fingers."

Lick.

"With my cock.*"

Lick.

"You want this just as fucking bad as I do, but you would rather lie to yourself and treat me like shit instead of admitting that you hate the life you're living back home, and you want to remember what this, *us*, feels like. Let me take care of you."

I fucking hope she wants to remember what we felt like, because I'm dying to remember. I pull back to admire what she's granting me. Her face is red with embarrassment and frustration as she waits for me to continue, crimson climbing up her neck, legs quivering as she tries to contain her arousal. It's obvious she's not getting what she needs from the man child she calls a fiancé, and I'm betting she hasn't been fucked well in a very long time. It's taking everything in me not to drop to my knees and taste her. She's had every chance to stop this, but she hasn't.

"So tell me, princess. Did I read that dirty little mind of yours?" I say with a grin on my face and an erection still bulging in my sweats.

She clears her throat trying to gather her composure, but she's not trying to get away from me. She didn't run away this time. We're getting somewhere.

"No, actually, you didn't. I was actually thinking about what an arrogant prick you are, and how I can't wait to get back to my life away from this boring little town, away from you. I was thinking about my fiancé who's waiting for me to come home. Oh, and I'm thinking about the fact that you need to learn to control that dick of yours since it seems to be trying to escape your pants all the damn time."

"Well, what do you fucking expect? I'm not blind, and this–" I gesture to my erection. "Well, any man would have to be blind to not get hard from the sight of you. You're too fucking gorgeous, and I can promise you that I'm not the only one who notices. Now as far as the rest of your fake thoughts, you mean the man you plan on marrying who can't even make you come? Who is too busy coming for his own pleasure to care about yours."

"How did you–" Her mouth slams shut when she realizes she slipped up, and just confirmed my accusation. I don't even try to contain the mischievous grin on my face as she glares at me. Not that I enjoy the fact that she's been denied the pleasure that she deserves, but it sure as fuck makes me happy that I'm giving her something she needs.

"It doesn't take a genius to figure it out, Tate. Only a woman who isn't getting pleased in her own bed would be clenching her thighs trying to ease the ache at the idea of getting to come repeatedly by another man's hand. And tongue. And cock."

The silence is only making the tension grow until her phone rings, breaking our eye contact as she reaches for it.

"Hey, Dad."

Charlie, you damn cockblock.

V

New Message — ↗ ×

To thirstwithclarissa@gmail.com

Smut

Dear Clarissa,

I am an avid smut reader. Lately I've started getting jealous of the female characters in my books because of their wild sex lives. The male characters are obsessed with them and can't keep their hands to themselves. My boyfriend isn't very touchy with me. When I told him I'd really enjoy it if he could be more like the males in my books (dominant, publicly affectionate, territorial) he told me that I'm being unrealistic by comparing him to fictional characters. Am I being unrealistic?

☺ 📎 Send

Chapter 15

Tatum

"No, no Dad, you *have* to come get me," I plead, checking to make sure I'm not dripping down my thighs. "It's after four. My flight is tomorrow night and I didn't fly all the way out here not to spend any time with you. And I'm getting stir crazy in this apartment. We're just watching TV. You said Jace was going to come get me!"

I swipe at a lone tear as it falls down my cheek hoping Asher isn't paying enough attention to notice. I allow myself a quick glance in his direction seeing his eyes staring directly at me as he leans against the doorframe of the hallway shoving his hands in his pockets. My frustration only grows when I see the smirk on his face like this is a stupid game for him.

"I'd rather you just come get me," I beg.

"I'm sorry honey. This is just out of my control. Your brother is staying with Kara for the rest of the weekend and my truck won't start. I'm sure Asher is taking good care of you in the meantime. He was always such a good kid."

My nose scrunches at the endearment coming from my dad's mouth about the man in front of me. Of course he still adores the guy like it hasn't been eight years since we broke up.

"Have him bring you home when the roads are clear. Be careful."

"Okay, Dad, I'll see you soon."

Tossing the phone on the couch, I stomp over to the window cursing mother nature for the white blanket that is the cause of my current predicament.

"Is there a problem?" Asher asks from behind me.

I wipe my eyes before turning to face him hoping he can't see the conflict painted on my face.

"Nope. I just need you to take me home. My dad can't get his truck to start now and my brother is too focused on getting laid to come get me."

I look at him pointedly hoping he gathers the fact that I'm insinuating the same thing about him.

"You offered to take me home last night, so it's not an issue now is it?"

"Of course not," he says smugly. "I'll take you home…when you admit I won the bet."

The blood drains from my face as I recall the words he whispered into my ear moments ago, my pulse spiking. This game of his is getting old, and the fact that my body is letting him think he's winning just pisses me off more.

"Over my dead body," I say.

He plops himself down on the couch not even glancing in my direction as he throws his legs up on the coffee table and leaning back with his arms behind his head.

"Well, it's either you admit I was right and I take you home when the roads are clear tonight, or you get comfortable and wait until someone comes to get you. So which is it, princess?"

"I'm not admitting a damn thing," I say, planting my feet firmly.

I'll be damned if he thinks he's going to manipulate the situation into something that it's not.

"Fine by me."

Standing up he tosses me my phone before heading down the hallway.

"Better get to calling people then. If you need me, I'll be in my room."

He throws me a wink over his shoulder before disappearing behind his bedroom door. What the fuck? I'm so sick of him toying with me, and I'm sick of playing into his twisted little mind game. One minute it feels like he's confessing all of his personal thoughts and feelings, bleeding his heart dry to me, and the next it just feels like he wants to fuck me so he can parade the trophy around for his buddies as they snicker about how he got between the legs of a desperate girl who was pining over her ex-boyfriend. I feel like we're eighteen again looking for ways to get under each other's skin.

Of course I'm not helping the situation by feeding into it, letting him see how my body reacts to his touch. And I fucking hate that I can't help how my skin erupts every time he touches me, like his caresses are burning through my flesh and permanently imprinting the feeling into my brain. But I'm a fucking idiot for thinking he actually still felt anything for me, like anything he said was real. I probably deserve it for how I left things so many years ago, but it doesn't soothe the sting that's burning my chest as I stare down his hallway.

Suddenly the pain in my chest turns from hurt to anger as I analyze the situation. What I did wasn't right, but what he's done since he saw me at the party, taunting me, is beyond wrong. I shouldn't still be paying the price for something I did when I was eighteen.

My fists clench at my sides as I start to shake with anger. He doesn't get to have the last word like that. I'm done being his entertainment. I let my legs carry me down the hall, mentally preparing myself for battle.

"You know what?" I say, shoving his bedroom door open causing it to slam against the wall. "I'm fucking sick of–"

Chapter 16
Asher

Just as my boxers hit the floor, the door flies open, Tate shouting, "I'm fucking sick of--"

And then open-mouthed silence.

She sees all of me now and not just my back in the dull moonlight. I could tell her I still love her. I could say, "I'm sorry I was screwing around with you." "I'm so glad you came home." "Be with me."

I could say so many sweet, romantic things, but instead my caveman brain has me stalking towards her saying "Sick of what, princess?"

"I- I'm- You-" she stammers.

"Sick of not letting yourself give in to what you've been thinking about since you saw me last night? Sick of not admitting how badly you wanted to rip off my clothes to see exactly what you're seeing now? Sick of denying that you still feel for me the way I feel for you? Because I'm sick of listening to you deny it, and I'm sick of wondering what those pretty pink lips taste like instead of actually finding out."

Almost instinctually she's darting her tongue out to wet her lips before pulling her bottom lip between her teeth and a blush is creeping up her neck.

Then, she takes a step forward.

"Fuck it," I hear myself saying.

I lunge forward as well, gripping her hair in my fingers pulling her mouth to mine. She moans into my mouth and I can feel her body giving into mine, melting in my hold. I pull back to trail rough kisses down her neck, feeling her pulse beating rapidly under her skin as I playfully bite just enough to leave a mark before moving down and sucking hard enough to leave another.

I tear my shirt off her shoulder and lick her skin, kissing the tender mark I just left. She cries out and I grab her thighs lifting her up and pinning her against the wall. Without hesitation, she throws her legs around me holding herself in place.

"Tell me to stop, princess, and I'll stop."

I don't fucking want to stop, but I won't force her if she stops this before it goes too far. She has to admit she wants this. I need to hear her say it.

"Don't call me a fucking princess," she pants, taking hold of my cock. "And don't you dare stop."

Chapter 17

Tatum

Don't you dare stop? Why did I say that? I know I should stop this. I should push him away and call everyone I can until someone agrees to come get me. I should be putting as much space as possible between us. I shouldn't be giving into his touch and letting my body melt in his hands as he kisses down my neck before taking my mouth, plunging his tongue in and claiming my mouth as his. But he was right about all of it. I need to know what he feels like. I need to remember.

And he needs to quit with the princess shit.

He growls, setting me down as he lowers to his knees doing exactly what he said I wanted him to. And fuck does he look amazing sinking to his knees with a sparkle in his eyes like he's worshipping me. He slides the shirt up slowly nipping at my inner thighs, soothing the skin with his tongue each time he bites. He locks his eyes on mine as he trails a finger across my slit, shooting me a satisfied grin when he finds me soaking wet with arousal just like he'd assumed, just like I've been the entire day. He brings his glistening finger to his mouth, groaning as he sucks it clean.

"Mmm. I was right after all," he purrs. "Nothing under this shirt, just waiting for me to taste you. And my fucking god do you taste sweet."

Without warning he's throwing my leg over his shoulder and greedily lapping at my wetness, circling my clit with his tongue, his fingers digging into my thigh keeping me in place.

"Oh fuck," I hiss.

He's built me up so much today that I was on edge before coming in here and I'm already close. I grip his dark hair in my fingers so hard that my knuckles turn white, riding his tongue as he inserts a finger while sucking on my clit. The stubble on his jaw rubs my inner thighs and I can't hold back the scream that erupts from my throat. I'm so fucking close. He adds a second finger and curls them just right, hitting me exactly where I need him to. I'm going to come.

"You taste so fucking good, baby," he murmurs as he pulls away just before I get the chance to come. By the look on his face he knows exactly what he's doing.

"Fucking asshole," I whimper in frustration.

"Don't worry, baby. You'll get what you want. But I'm taking my time with you. Eight fucking years, Tate. That's a long time to make up for. I'm going to savor every fucking second I get with you."

He picks me up like I weigh nothing and carries me to the edge of his bed. I can't help fisting his cock, pumping from base to tip.

I can see a drop of pre-cum, and I want to taste it. He gets off on my torture which only makes me want to get off on his. I sit up admiring the view of his body. This man is perfection in every sense of the word. I let my eyes travel from his muscular thighs up to his chiseled abs, then admiring the tattooed artwork that covers his sculpted arm before falling back down following the dark trail of hair leading down to his throbbing dick.

He's watching me with curiosity waiting for me to make my move. He isn't pushing me to do this, but I can tell the idea of me stopping this is killing him. Honestly the idea of stopping is killing me too. I lean in pressing a kiss to his stomach before taking his cock in my hand again, smiling when it elicits a drawn out moan from him as his head falls back.

Darting my tongue out, I lick the drop of cum off the tip before taking as much of him as I can into my mouth. He's bigger than I remember and I have to fight my urge to gag as I take him to the back of my throat. It's been a long time since I've given a blow job and I find that I'm self conscious about the idea that I may not be good at it anymore.

"Holy shit, baby. You have no idea how fucking good you feel."

His words give me the confirmation I need and I hum my appreciation and feel him jerk in my mouth. He likes that. I pop off and run my tongue from the base to the tip, not breaking eye contact when he looks down at me putting his hand on the back of my head gently coaxing me.

"Fuck, Tate. You can't look at me like that while you're sucking my cock unless you want me to lose it."

Smiling, I take him into my mouth again and look up at him through my lashes as I bob up and down taking him as deep as I can. Pushing me off of him he tosses me back on the bed crawling in between my legs burying his face in my neck.

"You're going to be the end of me."

"I need you, Asher," I beg. And I am fucking begging because the urge to feel him inside of me is overpowering any common sense telling me this is a bad idea.

"Spread those legs for me and let me taste how much you want me."

I shouldn't be embarrassed considering he already had me against the wall, but on the bed under these lights I don't want him seeing me, seeing my flaws. I'm bigger than I was in high school and my body has changed.

I shrink into myself and his head cocks to the side in a moment of confusion before he realizes what I'm thinking. He kisses me fiercely, possessively, sending tingles down my spine before pulling back and placing his thumb under my chin forcing me to look at him.

"Don't ever hide your body from me," he says, opening me up to him. "I want to see every inch of you. You have nothing to be ashamed of.

Look at my dick, Tate. Do you see how hard the sight of you makes me? I've been killing myself trying to restrain from fucking you senseless every time you looked at me. You're a fucking goddess who deserves to be worshipped, so let me worship you."

I let my legs fall open and he growls in appreciation before dipping down to kiss and nip at my thighs, peppering kisses on all of the spots that made me insecure several years ago. My heart lurches at the fact that he remembers those spots to a tee. He plunges two fingers in, curling them in the way he knows will break me.

"Come for me, baby," he says before sucking my clit into his mouth. My back arches and I'm clawing at his shoulders as fireworks explode behind my eyes and my orgasm takes over my body. He doesn't stop as I come down from my high even as I'm scooting up the bed pushing at his shoulders trying to escape his touch. It's too much.

"Give me another one," he demands grabbing my thighs pulling me back down the bed, lapping up every drop I give him.

"What? No, I can't." I whimper, his touch becoming so much it hurts my sensitive clit.

"You can and you will," he says before biting down on my clit hard enough to make me yelp. He withdraws his fingers and bites my thigh gripping onto my hips hard enough that I know he's leaving marks. Suddenly he's plunging his tongue inside me, consuming me, and pressing his thumb in circles against my clit. My pain erupts into another burst of pleasure as I cry out pressing my thighs against both sides of his head. I'm going to come again.

"That's it, princess. Give it to me," he says lapping up my mess.

"Don't" I murmur, his hair in my fists, "Call…" and my legs start to cramp. "Me" and electricity fills my body. "PRINCESS!" I scream, coming harder than I ever have that it almost borders being painful.

Panting, I pull him up to me watching as he wipes my wetness from his chin with the back of his hand. Usually, I would be embarrassed about it, but the look on his face is nothing but desire and satisfaction. His eyes gleaming with pleasure.

"I want you now. Please Asher. I need you."

"Say it again," he growls, climbing up my body to hover over me, staring at me like I'm his prey.

"Tell me what you want."

This man is trying to kill me. He's not going to give me what I want, what I need until I tell him explicitly. So much inspiration for my column. Time to take your own advice, Tatum.

"I want you to fuck me. I want to feel your cock inside of me. Now."

That must have been the permission he was looking for because he doesn't hesitate as he slams into me in one thrust making me cry out. I'm sensitive but the pain is mixing with pleasure as he thrusts in and out of me watching where he enters me.

"I wanted to take my time, but I can't keep my restraint with you. Do you have any idea how hard it's been not getting to satiate my hunger for you?"

He grabs my throat, putting pressure on both sides enough to allow air flow, but restrict it.

"It took every ounce of self control not to fuck you senseless when I saw you in my shirt this morning. I will never get enough of you. No matter how hard you try to fight me, I can't fight you anymore."

166

I don't have a chance to respond before he's flipping me over pushing my chest into the mattress, and pulling my ass up into the air, letting a hard smack fall on my right cheek before soothing it and slapping my other ass cheek hard enough to bring tears to my eyes. He wraps my braid around his hand and pulls causing my back to arch as he thrusts in, my clit pulsing with need even after coming twice. He's deeper in this position and I push myself back meeting him thrust for thrust. I can't get enough of this man, of this feeling, the reminder of what we felt like, only better.

"You feel so fucking good. I want to see you dripping with my cum."

I try to respond to his praise but I'm hit with another orgasm just as I feel him still inside me spilling his release.

He collapses on the bed next to me and we both lay panting in the mess we just made. I know I should say something, but I don't. I should feel guilty, but I don't. I know it'll make its impact soon enough, but for now, I resort to silence, basking in the ignorant bliss that I know is going to come crashing down.

Chapter 18
Asher

━━━━━━━━ ◦◆◦ ━━━━━━━━

I climb out of bed still reeling from what just happened. I walk to the bathroom to start the shower and stop when I walk back out to see her clutching the sheet to her body trying to cover herself as she searches for my shirt.

"What are you doing?"

She looks at me confused.

"Uh, getting dressed," she says, though it sounds more like a question than a statement.

I don't like the way she's covering herself like she's scared of me seeing her. As if I didn't just bury myself balls deep inside of her and kiss damn near every inch of her body, worshipping her like the fucking queen she is.

"No, you're not. Come shower with me."

I don't miss the slight grin that graces her face before it falls and her features are replaced with nervousness. Walking up to her, I grab the sheet and toss it to the floor, bending to my knees to get eye level with her.

She's looking at the floor so I grip the back of her neck, loving the feel of her tangled hair between my fingers. "I already told you," I say, forcing her to look at me, "You are fucking gorgeous. Every part of you. So I don't want you thinking for a second that you need to hide your body from me. I will remind you as many times as I need to until you believe me."

Fresh tears wet her eyes and I don't need to question her to know it's because she's not getting worshipped at home. I have to push down the anger that fuels me thinking about another man touching her, especially one that makes her question how beautiful she is. It makes me thankful that I get to be the one to show her though.

Grabbing her hand I pull her into the bathroom and check the water temperature before pulling her in with me. I caress her face letting myself focus on her features before pulling the hair tie from her braid, pulling it apart and tilting her head to wet her hair under the spray.

"I know this probably isn't girly enough for you, but it's all I've got."

She laughs as she reads the label of the two in one shampoo and conditioner I pour into my palm before scrubbing it into her scalp.

"If that shit makes my hair fall out," she says, her hands on mine, "I'm going to kill you. It's taken me forever to get it this long."

I can't help but admire the humor in her voice, but also know she would in fact kill me if her hair fell out.

"As long as I get to have you sit on my face first."

"Now that would kill you. Death by suffocation."

She's insulting her body again, but she's trying to play it off as a joke.

"You can suffocate me with that pussy any day of the week, baby. If I'm ever on death row, you'll be my last meal because I want to die with the taste of you on my tongue," I say as I take her mouth in a heated kiss. Her moan has my dick jerking back to life.

"How are you hard again?" she asks when she pulls back seeing my cock bobbing at full attention.

"I told you, princess, I mean goddess. I can't help the way I react to you. You're too fucking perfect." Not to mention the fact I gave myself blue balls all day by taunting her. A pang of guilt hits me as I think about how I toyed with her to get her to admit what we both knew knowing I probably was harsher than I should have been.

I take the body wash on a cloth and spread the lather over her body, focusing on all of my favorite parts. I smile when I see the slight bruises that are already starting to form on her hips, thighs, and neck. She'll have a hard time covering those and it makes my cock jerk in approval. I love marking her. Kneeling to wash her legs, I grip her calf placing it on my leg for balance, peppering kisses up the soapy trail to her center, ending with a light kiss to her swollen clit. I know she has to be sore so I don't plan on pushing anything else, but then she's fisting my hair in her fingers trying to push my head back to her pussy, throwing her head back against the wall.

"Please," she moans.

"Please what, baby? Tell me."

I hold back my chuckle at her frustrated groan. She's not one to vocalize what she wants, but I'm going to change that. I plan to give her the pleasure she's been denied for so long. I need to hear the words leave her pretty lips. I won't deny the fact that I'm a selfish bastard who loves hearing dirty words come from her mouth. She gets the hint when she looks down and meets my eyes realizing that I'm not moving.

"Please, Asher," she whimpers.

"All you have to do is ask, baby. I will never deny you. Just tell me," I tell her as I dip my head sucking her clit into my mouth before licking up her slit, tasting myself on her. This specific moment has me praising myself for investing in the apartment with the master bathroom suite, giving me plenty of room to have my way with her in the shower. Though if I had it my way, every spot in this apartment will be christened with her memory before I'm done.

I pull away and see the frustration fill her eyes as she groans, tightening her grip in my hair trying to keep me where she wants me.

"Tell me what you want, Tate."

Her silence only fuels me more as I plunge a single finger inside, curling it just right until she's squirming before pulling back again, leaving her wanting.

"You're a fucking asshole," she pants.

"Damn right. Always have been, always will be. Tell. Me. What. You. Want."

"I want–" Her eyes fly to the ceiling before clamping shut as she tries to find the courage to say the words I'm coaxing from her.

"No. Look at me and tell me."

I can't stop my grin as she groans in frustration finally giving up, shooting those soul snatching eyes at me.

"I want you to make me come!"

There it is, and my god hearing it is fucking glorious.

"Is that all?"

Her cheeks heat and I can tell there's more to that thought.

"No."

"What else do you want?"

Her eyes fill with desire as she dips to kiss me, clenching my hair before pulling back with a smile on her face.

"I want to suck you off until you can't stand anymore, and then I want to come on your dick."

Fucking hell. I was right. This woman is my undoing, and there is no coming back from the abyss that she just threw me in, and honestly I don't fucking want to come back. By the look on her face she knew exactly what that would do to me.

"I would love nothing more, baby," I say as I drop her leg to the floor, standing as she drops to her knees grabbing my throbbing dick and taking it into her mouth.

She licks up my shaft before taking me down her throat, suppressing a gag. She moans, and the vibration has me bracing myself on the shower wall. She looks up at me through wet lashes as she bobs up and down on my cock. The shower head spraying at just the right angle to cover her tits in water which is a glorious sight.

"Fuck, Tate. I can't last very long like this."

She pulls off, smiling up at me.

"Do something about it, or you're going to be coming down my throat."

I growl at her statement; her sudden confidence is a huge turn on.

"As much as I would fucking love to come down your throat, and I most definitely will be taking that offer, that's going to have to wait because I need to be inside of you again. I need to feel that tight fucking pussy come on my cock."

"Nobody's stopping you."

She stands, gripping my erection, pumping me in her hand. She is going to ruin me and I'm letting it happen. I sense her discouragement when I grab her wrist, releasing her hold on me to grab the handheld shower head and point it at her clit before dipping down to take a peaked nipple in my mouth.

"Make yourself come," I say handing her the shower head.

The brief look of shyness doesn't last as she takes it from me directing it where she needs. Seconds later her legs are starting to buckle as she struggles to keep herself up.

"That's it, baby. You are so fucking beautiful when you come," I praise her as I fist my cock in one hand, pumping slow enough to keep from coming, and grabbing onto her with the other.

"Holy shit," she says as she grips onto me while her orgasm takes over, racking her body. She drops the shower head as I grip her hips and pull her to me, devouring her in a kiss, ravaging her with my tongue, demanding more.

"You don't understand what you do to me, Tate," I whisper in her ear as I lift her leg, hitching it around my waist and position myself at her entrance, craving the sight of her pussy gripping me. We fit so perfectly together because she's my missing piece.

"I will never be able to get enough of you. You're fucking perfect," she moans as I bury myself as deep as I can, relishing in the feeling of her. Loving how her pussy is gripping me like a vice. I drive in fast and hard gripping her soapy hair in my fist forcing her eyes to mine.

"I want you looking at me when I come in your pussy."

She looks at me and I can't hold back anymore. Pressing my forehead to hers, I let go, enjoying the feel of her around me.

"You're mine Tate. Fucking mine," I say as I shudder my release inside of her.

As I pull out trying to gain my breath, anxiety takes over as I see the look in her eyes before she looks away. I can't tell if it's resentment, lust, anger, or a combination of them all. She's silent as she washes the rest of the shampoo from her hair and exits the shower, leaving me alone. *Shit.*

VI

New Message

To thirstwithclarissa@gmail.com

I cheated

Dear Clarissa,

I am engaged to a wonderful man I love. Recently I visited my childhood home and slept with my ex-boyfriend. Now I can't stop comparing them. I love that my fiancé is traditional and offers stability. He has our future planned out. I love that my ex is adventurous, doesn't care about what people expect of him, and is sexually generous. Am I just in a sex haze? Do I still marry my fiancé when I'm having so many doubts? Do I even deserve either one of them after lying and cheating?

Chapter 19
Tatum

You're mine. That's what he said.

It took me a minute to figure out if he'd said it out loud or if I had imagined it. The look in his eyes after the words left his mouth had me weak in the knees, but it also brought me back to reality. My blissful ignorance is gone as I throw my damp hair up in a bun and slip on my overly worn dress that I will have to throw away when I get home thanks to the memories that would flood my mind every time I looked at it. It took everything in me not to pull him to me and relish in the idea of being his again. A feeling I know all too well, and miss too much.

Guilt is eating me from the inside out as I grab my phone and see a few missed texts from Cayson. He is too good for me, and I know that I will never forgive myself for what I have done. I'm not a cheater. That's not the kind of person I am. I've always judged people for cheating, not understanding why you wouldn't end a relationship before jumping into bed with someone else. I'm to blame for the entirety of the shit show that is my life. I let this happen.

He told me to stop him and I didn't. Now the guilt is eating me alive as I realize the extent of the damage I have caused, the way I have hurt Cayson. The way that I could feel a fragment of Asher's heart break as I left the shower without any acknowledgement of the sentiment in his words. The way that I now feel as if I'm dying inside because all I wanted to do was return the sentiment and say the same words back.

"You know you owe me twenty bucks."

His statement jars me out of my head as I slip on a pair of his boxers and shimmy them up to hide under my dress. I know he senses I'm upset and his attempt at a joke just pisses me off more despite the fact that the only one I have a right to be angry with is myself.

"I need you to take me home. I leave tomorrow and I've spent almost my entire weekend with the one person I didn't want to see at all."

I can see the hurt in his eyes as I finally allow myself to look at him, and as I say the words, I instantly want to take them back, but I know I can't. The best thing for him is letting me go and watching me walk away. Again. I don't know how I'm going to survive it for a second time, but I know that his heart is too good for me.

"Are you saying you didn't enjoy it? You didn't want it?" There's a hint of anger in his voice now, but I can tell he wants a serious answer. He's afraid that I'm going to tell him he forced my hand.

"I'm saying I flew out here to spend time with my family, and instead have spent the majority of my time with you."

"So you're not denying you enjoyed it," he says with a slight grin as he wraps the towel around his waist and rummages through his dresser for a pair of boxers before dropping the towel and slipping them on. It takes every ounce of fight I have to keep from letting my eyes linger on his body.

"I'm saying I wasn't in my right mind. You knew that," I say, looking away because I can't see the resentment on his face without misty eyes. I'm lashing out at him because of my guilt, my irresponsibility and his hurt has me replaying that day in his bedroom eight years ago all over again. My heart shatters as I remember the hurt that took place in that room and clearly never healed for either of us.

"So you're saying I took advantage of you? That's what you're saying?" I hear a slight crack in his voice at the idea that he forced me into something I didn't want, and my guilt continues to grow.

"Fuck. No. That's not what I mean. I'm just saying neither of us was sober."

He scoffs as he throws on a pair of boxers and towel dries his hair.

"We knew what we were doing. You went with it. I told you to tell me if you wanted me to stop. And for the record, you used to consider me family, too, you know."

He's right. I used to consider him my family because I loved him just as much as family. He was my home a long time ago, and in this moment I really wish I could throw myself into his arms and let him be my sanctuary, my home again.

"This isn't a fucking game, Asher! This is real life. You tormented me, taunted me all day and then you claim me like I'm your property."

He crosses the room, placing his hand on my cheek, and I catch myself melting into his touch before pulling away, his eyes full of honesty as he looks at me. I don't mean it. In fact I wanted to stay in that moment forever listening to his words on repeat. But I know I can't.

"I know this isn't a game," he says, his voice sincere. "I'm sorry for screwing with your head, okay? I just needed you to admit that you were harboring feelings for me, too. You're not my property, but I sure as hell did enjoy treating you like you were mine again."

"Please, Asher," I whisper, turning to walk away. "We're not going to do this." I feel his presence follow closely behind. I know he likely isn't going to let me get away that easily, but I have my hopes.

"Do what?" he asks at my back.

"Pretend like everything is fine. Like we're fine."

"Ignorance is bliss, right?" Talk about my own words biting me in the ass.

"No, Asher. It isn't, and I can't fucking do this. Just leave it alone."

He grabs my wrist, spinning me to face him and the words fall from my lips as fresh tears roll down my cheeks.

"I can't fall for you again," I tell him. "I'm going back to Florida, you're going back to California, and I'm getting married in three weeks. As far as I'm concerned, this never happened."

Not that I will ever be able to forget that it happened, and don't want to. But those are the words he needs to hear to let this go. I don't have much fight left in me.

"Are you fucking kidding me?" he says, almost yelling. "You're going to walk down the aisle to that douche and just pretend we didn't have the most mind blowing sex? That you didn't feel that connection, that spark like eight years haven't passed without each other?"

"Exactly, Asher. It was sex. That's it. And Cayson isn't a douche; you haven't even met him," I hiss through the tears, trying to gather every bit of venom I have left to throw at him.

He grabs my face wiping them from my cheeks. He can see right through me, but I refuse to admit what he wants. I can't.

"I don't have to meet him to know he's a douche. I can tell he doesn't make you happy, and that's enough. It wasn't just sex, and you know it. You felt what I did."

"Which was what, Asher?"

"We went right back to where we were eight years ago. It was like no time had passed. We work perfectly together even if you don't want to admit it. We make each other happy, we heal the brokenness in each other but you're just fighting it."

The longing in his eyes is just making my guilt hit me harder, and I know I can't give him what he's fighting for. I made that choice eight years ago when I ran away. He does make me happy, but I can't reciprocate it the way he deserves.

"What do you expect me to do, Asher? Call Cayson and tell him I fucked my ex-boyfriend and the wedding is off?"

The way he's eyeing me tells me he doesn't think it's an improbable idea. I'm sure if he thought I would do it, he'd dial the number for me.

"You want me to confess my love to you and just pretend like eight years haven't passed of us living our separate lives?" I continue. "You want me to fall for you all over again and act like I don't remember how bad we were for each other? I built a life after you, one without you in it. Do you expect me to just leave all of that behind? I can't Asher."

"You can't what?" he asks as I pull from his grip and walk to the living room. He keeps dragging the words out of me, and I keep letting him even though it's killing me.

"I can't love you again." My voice cracks through the tears.

Asher brushes past me, snatching his keys from the counter.

"I'll take you home. The roads should be clear enough by now," he says as he grabs a hoodie from a chair and slips on his shoes. He's out the door not bothered by the fact that he's in his boxers, leaving the door wide open before I can say anything else. Sniffling, I wipe the tears from my eyes and walk out to his car, bracing myself against the freezing cold and a shattered heart.

The ride to the house is silence apart from the quiet whir of the heat blasting through the vents. As he pulls into the driveway, I don't bother looking at him before reaching for the door handle. I don't have a chance to get my legs out before he's reaching over me pulling my door shut, locking me in with him.

"You may not be able to love me anymore Tate, but–" He takes a deep breath, looking away from me like he's debating if he should finish his thought. "Fuck. Damn it." He runs his hands down his face before turning to me.

"But what?" I ask as my pulse starts hammering in my chest. I know I shouldn't let him say whatever he's going to, but I need to hear it even if I can't return them.

"I can't stop loving you." His admission is just barely above a whisper, and his eyes show nothing but truth to his words. He means it.

I'm fumbling for words trying to think of a response, but he beats me to it.

"I never got over you. I tried for years. I buried my thoughts of you in booze and random women hoping to dull the ache of the crater sized hole you left in my chest when you ran away. I thought I had finally convinced myself that you were wrong for me, and that I hated you for leaving the way that you did. But then I saw you at that fucking party. I wanted to treat you like shit for what you did. I wanted to keep believing that I wasn't still madly in love with you. But fuck, Tate. I can't stop. I can't stop remembering how much I loved being with you, how you were it for me. You were the only thing in my life that I was scared to lose. I hate what you did, but I don't hate *you*. We could've talked it out. We could've figured out how to make it work. You had my heart in your hands and you fucking mutilated it, but I never stopped loving you."

I open my mouth to speak but he stops me, grabbing my face with both hands willing me to look at him.

"You can't deny that it felt right in that bed. It felt right when I was inside of you, and you know it. We felt like us again. Fucking someone you hate doesn't feel like that. You don't get off on coming on the tongue of someone you hate. You still have feelings for me even though they might be buried because you refuse to admit they still exist. You are better than every other fucking woman out there, and you know that guy isn't right for you. You don't want to marry him. You're settling because you want the white picket fence life and he's offering it to you, but you are sacrificing everything else with it. You aren't happy, and I can fucking see it on your face. But you were happy every second I was inside of you, every second that I was with you. You were happy spending time with me even if you don't want to admit it. For a split second I had my girl back. I saw it in your eyes in the shower when I said you were mine. I can't get over you, Tate. I just can't."

I am at a complete loss of words for the confession that just rolled off his tongue. He lets go of my face and pulls back, waiting for my reply. There's a slight gloss to his eyes and I know he means every word of what he said. He still loves me, and he's right about all of it. I know I still love him, but I'm denying myself that right. I don't get to love him anymore. We became different people after that day in his bedroom. There is a huge secret that he doesn't know about, and I can't dig up that part of my past. It's too painful, and it would do nothing to help either of us. It would only cause more hurt.

Seeing the hope in his eyes is killing me. If my shattered heart feels anything like it did for him when I walked out of his life, I can't forgive myself for what I did. I know now I was a hypocrite for leaving based on his lie when I was keeping something much bigger. He deserves so much more than I have offered him–or can offer him. I have a life back home I have to go back to. The life I chose for myself instead of a life with him. He has a life in California that has nothing to do with me. He's going to become an attorney at the law firm and fulfill his potential, becoming the man I always knew he could be. Even if I wanted to admit that there's still something, I can't ask him to give up his life, not again. He finally grew up and made something of himself. I couldn't be with him knowing I was holding on to a broken piece of my life that he can't know about.

He takes my hand in his, placing a kiss on each of my knuckles as he waits for me to sort my thoughts. His patience is excruciating as I accept that I am the only one to blame for everything that has led up to this point. He was given an opportunity that he *had* to take, and I hated him for keeping it from me as I stood there carrying a much bigger secret. A secret I lost. A secret I never got to tangibly hold, but will always hold room for in my heart.

Suddenly my heart aches as I picture what it would've been like if I had come clean in his room. The outcome may have stayed the same, but I could've had him with me as I went through the heartbreak in that hospital room. I will never be whole again, and I can't give him what he wants. So the best thing I can do is hit him where it hurts so he does hate me. So he can have the life he deserves, void of any love for me and my broken mind.

I pull my hand from his and grab the handle, swinging the door open. I swallow the lump growing in my throat and will the tears to stay at bay as I look at him and say everything I don't truly mean.

"Well, Asher, I guess you just have to figure it out. Stop loving me. I will *never* be the Tate that you remember. There will never be an us again. We fucked and that was it. I'm going back to Florida where my life and my *home* is, and you can go back to California and leave your fantasies of whatever you thought we could be behind."

I grab my clutch from the floorboard remembering that I left it in here Friday night, too drunk to care. I rummage through it, grabbing what I need and slap it in his hand. Climbing out of the car I let the tears fall as I watch him crumple the twenty dollar bill in his fist and drive off leaving me clutching my arms to my chest in the cold.

I fucking hate Michigan.

Chapter 20
Asher

◆

I knew she was trying to hide her tears as she got out of the car. She's never been good at hiding her feelings from me, and that hasn't changed. I'm not an idiot, and I know she didn't mean what she said as she let me leave her standing there in the cold as a sob racked her body.

I meant every word I said to her. I did want to hate her for running away. Not that she can be completely to blame for the situation. It took me a while to come to terms with it, but I fucked up too. I should have just told her when I got the offer. But I can't make her admit what we both know. If she wants to lie to herself and pretend I still mean nothing to her, then I'm not going to stop her. I poured my heart out to her in that car and she couldn't get the nerve to admit what she felt. At least that's what I'm trying to tell myself to make me feel better because admitting to myself that she feels nothing at all for me is more pain than I want to feel right now.

She didn't know that I thought about a future with her: a marriage, and maybe even a kid or two. I didn't want her holding on to false hope. I was young and so fucking stupid. I didn't know if I'd ever actually be willing to fully commit and settle down. But if I had ever been ready for that commitment, it would have been with her because, fuck, that woman could talk me into anything if it meant putting a smile on her face. I was two seconds from telling her to marry me. And now I hate myself for spilling everything I did to her. Again, I let her hold my heart in her hand, and again she mutilated it. She let me bleed out in that car.

✛

I needed a drink after the disaster that was fucking sappy Asher so now I'm slouched on the couch in my sister's living room sipping on a glass of whiskey. She always did have a good taste in alcohol, and if there's anyone who's going to let my tipsy ass spew my bullshit without judgement, it's Ari.

"I don't know what to do, Sis." I throw my head back staring at the ceiling as I savor the burn of the liquor warming my body, numbing the ache in my heart just a little bit.

"What do you mean, you don't know what to do? You love her, do you not?" she asks as she swirls the ice in her glass finishing off her amaretto sour. She's on her third one since I've been here. Lush.

"You fucking know I do. But she clearly doesn't feel the same way, or she is too comfortable with living a life that she hates. Either way, it doesn't matter. It's clear where we stand in her head. Not to mention she's getting married in three weeks."

"You are such a dumbass," Ari says as she throws a pillow at me, spilling some of my remaining whiskey onto the couch.

"What the fuck. How am I dumbass?"

"If you seriously can't tell that she's in the same position as you, then you are just as ignorant and oblivious as most men I wasted my time on."

"Not you, baby," she coos at her fiancé–dammit, I forgot his name again–who's glaring at her over his phone from his spot on the other side of the room, clearly not interested in our conversation.

"She is not in the same position as me. She's getting married in three weeks to someone who isn't me. She's got her life planned out, and I am clearly not in it. She was pretty clear about how she feels in the car."

"For fucks sake, Asher. Do I seriously have to spell it out for you?"

She takes my silence as her answer as she shifts in her seat.

"Remember that her and I were pretty close a long time ago. I think my stubbornness rubbed off on her." She winks and smiles at me before continuing: "She's obviously still in love with you, but doesn't know how to accept it, so she's using this wedding as her excuse. You weren't ready to admit that you would permanently commit to her eight years ago, but now you are. Did you really expect her to get a taste of your dick again and just give up on everything she knows?"

Liam chuckles, and I don't know if it's at Ari's question or something on his phone.

"I–" My statement is cut short as she continues.

"She still has no idea that you'd be willing to make that full commitment to her, so why would she give up her entire life for a risk that you'll never give her what she needs?"

I find myself enamored by the logic leaving my little sister's mouth. I'm realizing now I don't give her enough credit.

"If she came in here right now," she goes on, "and told you she'd leave Cayson if you'd agree to marry her, would you?"

"I'd drop to my knee on the fucking spot."

I shock myself with how easy it is to admit. The smile on my sister's face tells me she knew exactly what she was doing, and she's satisfied with my answer.

"But she doesn't know that. In her eyes, you are still the eighteen-year-old who broke her heart. You are the idiot boy who had no true ambitions other than traveling and getting your dick wet when she'd let you."

I go to speak but she lifts her eyebrow like she's challenging me to say otherwise. I opt for staying quiet since she's right.

"She needs you to show her that she is enough for you to forget what you always said about never wanting more. You know that woman. She

186

needs the wife title. Maybe kids are in your future, maybe they aren't. If you aren't willing to show her how serious you are about giving her the commitment she's always wanted, then you should let her go. She deserves all of you or none of you."

I huff out a breath because I hate how right she is.

"When did you become so fucking wise?"

She chuckles. "I've always been smarter than your stubborn ass, three year difference or not."

"So what am I supposed to do?" I check the time on my phone. "She's already at the airport. So what, am I supposed to drop everything and fly to Florida? Give up my life in California and confess my undying love for her at the wedding as I ask her to leave him for me? Pretend that she didn't just rip my heart out and let me walk away?"

"I'm not saying to wait until the pastor tells everyone to speak now or forever hold their peace and drop to your knees begging her to take you back, but I am saying she isn't married *yet,* and you still have the power to do something. Whether she does anything with it is up to her."

She straightens and looks me dead in the eyes.

"You haven't loved anyone else in the eight years that she's been gone, Ash. She was it for you and we both know it. I think she does too, but she's scared to admit it. I'm not saying how she handled your confession was right, or that she wasn't in the wrong for leaving you the way she did after graduation, but you owe it to both of you to at least try. Give it your all before you give up."

"Is anyone else hungry?" Liam asks without looking up from his phone.

187

Chapter 21
Tatum
Two weeks later

⋅◆⋅

This is not fucking happening. No way this is fucking happening right now. I bring the stick up to my face for the fiftieth time hoping my eyes have been deceiving me for the past twenty minutes. Nope. There's no denying that second blue line. Fuck me. Actually, don't because that's how I got into this situation. Shit.

I run my hands over my face in the hopes that when I open my eyes again, I will wake myself up and there won't be three positive pregnancy tests on the bathroom counter mocking me, judging me, guilting me. Except when I will myself to open my eyes again, there are in fact three positive tests sitting right in front of me. I am not dreaming, this is really happening. I'm pregnant.

Tears start clouding my vision as my reality finally sets in and the shock wears off. I drop down to the floor trying to reel in the panic flooding my veins as my body is racked with sobs. I'm scared. I'm hurt. I'm guilty. My chest heaves from my crying and I barely make it to the toilet as my stomach empties it's entire contents from the day which isn't much since I've been feeling like shit this past week. That should have been my first clue. I don't get sick, but for the past week my head has been pounding and my stomach has been in knots. Not to mention the mood swings. My dumb ass just assumed it was because of the chaos that had ensued in my life, and the upcoming wedding. But when I realized it was time for my monthly test, the chaos continued tenfold. This wasn't supposed to happen. I have an IUD, and I haven't had a scare one time since I've had it. My periods are still irregular and have been since my miscarriage so I take pregnancy tests regularly just to make sure. Cayson and I never use condoms, but he always pulls out. And considering we haven't had sex for almost two months, it doesn't take a genius to connect the dots. I'm pregnant with Asher's baby. Again.

I've been avoiding Cayson as much as possible since I got home. My brain couldn't handle my emotions, and the idea of being with him intimately was totally off-putting. Not only because I feel guilty for cheating on him with Asher, but also because I've never felt the way with Cayson that I did with Asher. He made me feel so wanted, sexy, desired. It was like he couldn't get enough of me.

To my surprise, Cayson's clinginess has faded drastically since my return. He seems different. But then again, it could just be me because I am most definitely different. At first when I got the positive test, I hoped for everyone's sake that it was Cayson's. It would make everything easier even though my guilt would remain. But as I played the timeline in my head, I knew it was impossible. I had my period the week before I left for Michigan which meant this baby is definitely Asher's.

My brain is spinning with a million thoughts. The fear and pain I went through with my miscarriage is something I would never wish on anybody, and I can't go through that again. I place my palms to my stomach picturing the baby I lost and wondering what they would have looked like. I imagine what this baby will look like, and pray that I get to see their face, get to hold their tiny frame in my arms as I count their fingers and toes. I grip the toilet again as another dry heave takes over my body.

I let the guilt take over as I lay on the floor because I know I did this to myself. I allowed this to happen. I haven't spoken to Asher since he dropped me off at my house two weeks ago. I couldn't let myself fall into that heartache again. The heartache that was my relationship with Asher. I knew we could never be the same after what happened what now feels like eons ago. I couldn't come clean with him about the miscarriage, and I couldn't live with the guilt of seeing his face every day, loving him, letting him love me, and keeping it from him. I have no doubt I am still madly in love with him, and he was right about everything he said.

I know that I am a fraud for coming back to my fiancé with a smile on my face continuing with our wedding like nothing happened. Asher and I weren't supposed to happen. I can't uproot everything I've built over a stupid drunken hookup that I'm sure Asher regrets at this point. Call me an irresponsible bitch all you want. I have to follow through with this wedding. As wrong as it is, I need stability in my life. I need safety. Asher isn't a safe choice, but Cayson is. For the sake of this baby, I need safe.

It's at this moment I am so thankful for waiting to move in together until after the wedding so I have a space to myself to think without worrying about when he'll be home. I just have to think. I've tried my best to keep my composure around Cayson since I came back. He was angry about my lack of communication while I was gone, but not nearly as mad as I had expected. We talked it out and I have tried to act as normal as possible while finding excuses to keep our time together minimal, walking on eggshells to make sure I don't slip up. Luckily he's been hanging out with some friend of his a lot lately after work so I haven't had to entertain him as much.

I'm pacing back and forth in the bathroom when my phone rings. Cayson's face pops up on my screen and I have to calm my nerves before picking up. I know he's likely calling to verify our plans for tonight that I reluctantly agreed to.

"Hey, babe, what's up?" I ask, hoping he doesn't hear the hoarseness in my voice from crying.

"Hey, I just wanted to call and let you know I have to cancel on our dinner plans tonight."

"Oh. That's okay. Why do you have to cancel?" I can hear a hushed voice in the background but I can't make out what they're saying.

"Just work stuff. I won't bore you with the details," he says followed by a... *is that a giggle?* "Anyway, I just wanted to let you know, so you're free to do whatever you want to do."

Something in the back of my mind tells me to press him for details, but the nausea in my stomach pushes it out of the way and gives thanks for the exit from tonight's dinner that undoubtedly would have ended up in my toilet before night's end.

"Ok. I'll probably just have a comfy night in. Watch some movies or something."

I pause before I say the words that have suddenly become acid on my tongue every time I say them: "I love you."

Silence lingers on his end of the phone before he replies with a quick "You, too."

The line goes dead and I let out a heavy sigh as the guilt comes back to eat my mind. I'm getting married in five days and I'm pregnant with my high school lover's baby. What the fuck is my life?

Heading to the kitchen, I grab a pint of cookie dough ice cream from the freezer before plopping on the couch to eat my feelings and rid my mouth of the vomit taste lingering in my throat. The idea of sleeping with Cayson and lying about the timeline of my pregnancy crosses my mind and I allow it briefly before I throw the idea out the window. I'm fucked up for staying with him knowing what I did, but I'm not fucked up enough to make him think he knocked me up. I'll find a way to tell him after the wedding. I need some time to think things through before I make any rash decisions that could ruin my relationship and my life.

"We'll figure it out. I promise. No matter what, you'll be okay," I say to the small life now growing in my body as I shovel another bite of ice cream into my mouth before suddenly being repulsed by the taste and throwing it back in the freezer.

It's moments like this I wish I had a best friend to run to for advice. My stomach curls as I'm reminded I've only had one best friend in my life and he's states away, living a life that has nothing to do with me, that can have nothing to do with me. I know I'll have to tell Asher at some point. If last time taught me anything, it's that he deserved the truth no matter what the outcome may have been. But that point is not now, and I have to make sure I can salvage my soon to be marriage first. After the honeymoon, I'll figure out a way to tell Cayson and convince him our marriage is worth it whether I believe that or not. Asher can wait.

Chapter 22
Tatum

A few days have passed, but my guilt and nausea have not. Every day, my trips to the toilet to hurl are a constant reminder of what happened in Michigan. Memories keep flooding my mind. Memories of how it felt to be around him again, how my body reacted to his every touch, how alive I felt when he kissed me, and how he made me come harder than I ever have. I tried to be angry with myself for the first day, but I couldn't find a way to be angry. How can I be angry about something that gave me the blessing growing inside of me? The fear that telling Cayson will make him leave and the guilt for following through on this wedding are still very prominent though.

Asher may have admitted he still loves me, but that doesn't mean he is willing or ready to be a father, or a husband. For all I know, it was a post orgasm high. I still have no idea how this is going to work, but I know that no matter what, my baby is going to be loved and cared for even if it ends up just being the two of us against the world. My first appointment is in three weeks right after we get back from the honeymoon in Bora Bora. I figure it's best to make sure everything is okay first before I open my mouth about any of it. I've taken a pregnancy test every day since I found out just so I can see the line get darker, the trauma of my miscarriage trying to rob me of my hopes for a healthy pregnancy.

With the wedding only two days away, I have made the concrete decision to still get married and face the consequences after the fact. The twisted part of my brain is using the logic that once we're married, Cayson won't leave. I know how disgusting that decision is, and I'm sure there's a reservation at a table in hell with my name on it.

My mind is telling me that Asher won't want to be a dad, especially after the way I left him heartbroken in my dad's driveway, even as my heart aches with the hope that he would take on the role without hesitation. I saw the hurt in his eyes as I slammed the door. The hurt that diffused into anger as he felt my betrayal all over again. I ran away from him for a second time because I won't admit the truth to myself. I refuse to admit that I still love him, and wish we could have the life I've always dreamed of. Both of us sitting on the swing on our front porch watching our kids run through the yard playing with the dog that we let them talk us into. I refuse to let myself imagine the scenarios that I know will never be possible with Asher because of the decision I made eight years ago to run away from my problems instead of fighting for them.

Cayson would be a good father figure. He's got a stable life and he's always wanted kids. He does so well with his nephews when they're around. As much as I considered calling off the wedding, I couldn't do it. Visions of my childhood growing up without both parents always present had me throwing that idea out the window. I will be a kick ass mother all on my own if it comes to that, but I don't want it to. I know both of my parents love me and did their best to provide for me, but that didn't stop the hurt I felt when I had to jump back and forth between them instead of getting them both at the same time.

Asher has finally gotten what he wants out of life in a state across the country from me. I won't ask him to give that up, and I'm not willing to give up what I've built here which is a stable and safe space that can provide for a child.

One thing I don't remember having in my first few weeks with my first pregnancy is the horniness. I just want sex all the damn time. I don't know how I haven't broken my vibrator from the amount of use it's had in the past three days. As I lay in bed willing for sleep to take me, that feeling won't go away. I can't stop fidgeting in the sheets as my body craves release. Giving in, I reach into my bedside drawer and grab my vibrator for the thirteenth time this week. Slipping it down my shorts, it only takes a few minutes to realize it isn't enough. I can't clear my head. I will an orgasm to give me the release I need to be satiated so I can sleep, but the pressure on my clit isn't doing it for me. I let out an aggravated huff and close my eyes letting my imagination take my mind wherever it needs to go to achieve my climax.

I turn up the vibration and insert a finger, pumping slowly as visions take over my thoughts. Memories. The way Asher's fingers traced up and down my thighs as he worshipped my body. I imagine his finger's pumping inside of me as I move mine faster. I clench my eyes shut even harder as I remember the feeling of his tongue circling my clit as he told me to come on his tongue. I remember the feeling of being stretched as he shoved his cock inside of me, his ruthless way of fucking me as he claimed my body in a way I hadn't experienced. I know now he was trying to claim me, mark me as his in a way nobody else could. I remember the gratifying feeling of looking in the mirror the next day and seeing the bruises his fingers left behind from grabbing me so roughly. Those were a pain in the ass to cover up, for the record. I turn the vibrator up again and press it firmly to my clit as I insert another finger and curl them trying to achieve the way it felt when it was Asher's fingers that were fucking me.

"Oh fuck."

I writhe in the sheets tossing my head back and forth as I replay every kiss, every touch he gave me in his apartment. *You're mine.* Remembering those words as he whispered them in my ear, letting go as he came inside of me has me gasping for air as the orgasm finally takes over, racking my body.

But too quickly it's over, the orgasm ending and yet again, I am not satisfied. The visions of Asher fade away as I pull the covers over my head and allow the tears to flow because I know no matter what I do, I will never be satisfied the way I was in his apartment. The way I was when I felt happy and cared for. Desired. I allow myself to grieve for the future I gave up when I walked away as sleep finally takes over.

VII

New Message — ↗ ✕

To   thirstwithclarissa@gmail.com

Please help

Dear Clarissa,
My boyfriend and I are long distance. Recently I've been trying to increase the intimacy within our relationship. I'm really shy and struggle with confidence but I decided to try sexting. I sent a few pictures that I felt really good in and my boyfriend ignored them. When I finally asked him about it he just said they were nice. It makes me feel insecure like he doesn't find me attractive anymore. I don't know how to keep our sex life alive with so much distance between us. How do I talk to him about it?

☺   📎   **Send**

Chapter 23
Tatum

◆◆◆

The sun shines through my window and I roll over, cursing into my pillow. I fucking hate mornings. I grab my phone from the night stand and see a missed text from Cayson. *I'll meet you at your mom's at 10.* Shit. I forgot that I told him we could meet my mom for brunch at her house today before the rehearsal dinner. It was her suggestion, though I'm not sure why she couldn't just wait to see us tonight. Part of me assumes it's because she knows Dad is flying in today and she's trying to avoid being roped into seeing him.

I rub the sleep from my eyes and drag myself to the bathroom to shower before having a cup of apple juice for breakfast. My morning sickness –which I thought wasn't supposed to happen until like six weeks by the way– is terrible and I know I probably won't be able to keep much food down today, but I'm hoping any urgent trips to the bathroom can be explained away as wedding jitters because that's not a total lie.

As soon as I pull up to my mom's house I instantly regret agreeing to come. I feel like shit, and the bags under my eyes are evidence that I haven't been sleeping. I'm not stupid enough to think my mom won't make a comment about it. Cayson's car is already parked in front of the garage so I reluctantly make my way to the front door, popping a mint in my mouth to cover my vomit breath.

I ring the doorbell and a few seconds later Mom is opening the door with a smile that falls the instant she takes in my appearance.

"My word Tate, have you even slept at all? You look terrible."

Told you.

She grabs my shoulders and pulls back raking her eyes over me and I feel like I'm being inspected.

"I'm fine, Mom. It's just wedding stress," I say shrugging her off, walking into the kitchen with her trailing behind me.

There's a ridiculous spread of food on the counter considering it's only for the three of us, but I'm not surprised. That woman can't do anything in a simple manner. My mouth waters when I see a plate of homemade cinnamon rolls next to a platter of mixed fruits. My empty stomach is growling at the sight and I don't hesitate to grab two plates, filling them with fruit, a cinnamon roll, two slices of quiche, three finger sandwiches, and cubed cheese before grabbing a bottle of water and taking it to the dining room.

"Seriously, Tate, what has gotten in to you this morning?" she asks as I shove a strawberry in my mouth.

"What?" I ask, my mouth still full of food. I try not to laugh at her when she looks at me with pure disgust that I'm not acting proper.

"You could at least wait until we're all seated to start eating. And you don't need to eat like this is your last meal."

"Well, where is Cayson anyway? I got here last so you both could've been ready to eat when I got here."

"He's um, he's in the bathroom, I think," she stutters.

I narrow my gaze at her as I hear footsteps approaching.

"Hey, babe," Cayson says as he walks across the room leaning down to plant a kiss on my cheek. The feeling sending shivers through my body, and not the good kind.

"The food looks great, doesn't it? Mia is a master in the kitchen."

I refrain from rolling my eyes at his praise because the cinnamon roll I'm shoving into my mouth is fucking heavenly I have to admit. Swallowing my bite of food, I smile at both of them.

"The food is amazing, Mom. Thank you for cooking."

I scoot my chair back and make my way back to the kitchen.

"Come on, make your plates so we can eat together," I call over my shoulder.

They eye each other as they enter the kitchen grabbing a plate and silently filling them with food.

Smiling at Cayson, I follow him back into the dining room. He sits in the chair across from me, my mother next to him.

"So rehearsal starts at 5 and dinner is right after. I called the restaurant and double checked the reservation so everything is good to go. But Tate, please don't eat like you're eating right now. I think you should go light on breakfast tomorrow too so you're not bloated trying to fit in your... *dress*."

"Sure thing," I say as I smile and shove another piece of cinnamon roll into my mouth.

"Do you want me to pick you up from your place and drive you to rehearsal?" Cayson asks, pushing food around his plate with his fork.

"No, it's okay. I will meet you there. I'm going after my nail appointment so I'll head there when I'm done."

My mom smiles and I can tell it's because she's looking at my nails, happy that I'm doing something to them instead of leaving them bare as they are.

After we eat, and, luckily for me, a very light discussion, we carry our dishes to the sink and Cayson leads me to the front door, giving me a kiss before leaving. Something about picking up his boutonniere, I guess. I'm about to make my getaway too when my mom calls from the kitchen.

"Tatum, come in here and help me clean up before you go, please."

At least she said please for once.

I walk in the kitchen dragging my feet, suddenly feeling my nausea starting to creep in. I'm regretting filling my stomach with food trying to think of an excuse to leave before I get roped into cleaning.

"I'll wash, you dry," she says as she gestures to the hand towel on the counter. Damn it.

"You really didn't have to do all of this for brunch, Mom. It was just the three of us. Not that I'm complaining about the food because it was delicious, but you don't have to make everything extravagant. You're allowed to go simple once in a while."

She snorts as if the word simple is an insult.

"You know Cayson hasn't complained one time about the wedding. Yet all you've done since the start is complain. He is trying to give you everything you've wanted and you don't seem very grateful."

Guilt filters through my brain because I know she's right.

"You're right, Mom."

Her eyes shoot to mine, eyebrows raised at my confession.

"I haven't been fair to Cayson, with everything really," I admit. "I've taken advantage of him and everything he has to offer. He's giving me the white picket fence life just like I have always wanted. He treats me well and he wants to make me happy. He is the definition of everything you told me to wait for, and now I have it. Thank you for making me realize the amazing future he's giving me."

Even as I say the words I can't get myself to believe them. The first part is true, but I'm struggling with the last of it. Her hands are frozen in the sudsy water, staring at the sink like it's on fire and she doesn't know how to put it out.

"That's wonderful. I'm glad you're seeing what a great man Cayson is."

Her knuckles go white as she grips the plate in her hand so hard I'm convinced it's going to shatter.

"Mom?"

"Hmm?" She looks at me like she's pondering something.

"Are you okay?"

She rinses off the plate and hands it to me like nothing happened.

"I texted the wedding planner to make sure she's going to be there before one tomorrow," she says, grabbing another dish from the water. "That gives us enough time to get ready, but allows extra time to go over everything before the ceremony."

Her phone pings from the counter.

"Oh, that's probably the wedding planner. Can you check that for me?" she asks, holding up her soap covered hands.

"Sure."

I walk over to the counter to pick up her phone swiping up on the screen, not paying attention to the number displayed.

"Oh my God! What the fuck?" The phone falls from my hand as my mom whirls around flinging water everywhere, her eyes wide with panic.

"What? What is it?"

She goes to reach for her phone but I snatch it from the floor and clutch it to my chest before she has a chance.

"What the hell is your problem, Tate?" she asks, grabbing a hand towel to dry her hands.

I pull the phone back enough to make sure I saw the message correctly. The screen is cracked, but I can still see it clear as day. For a second I'm convinced I'm dreaming as I look at the screen because there's no way it's real. *I miss you already,* sits in the blue text bubble above a picture of an erect penis poking through the zipper of jeans. Cayson's jeans.

Mom lunges for her phone, but I clutch it to my chest keeping her from getting it.

"For the love of God, Tate, give me my phone."

With shaking fingers I delete the message before handing it over to my mother.

"What? There's nothing on here? And you're paying to fix this screen," she says as she scrolls through looking for the evidence that I just deleted.

"Nothing. I'm sorry. I just got shocked when I picked up your phone. I'm sorry I dropped it. I'll pay to fix it."

"My phone shocked you?" she asks, still scrolling through her phone clearly not buying my excuse.

"Yeah, weird huh?"

Seconds later my stomach doles out it's regular reminder of my body's current status and sends my food flying up my throat as I scramble for the toilet. I empty my breakfast into the bowl before rinsing my mouth and walking back into the kitchen where my mom is propped up against the kitchen counter staring at me. For a second I convince myself she can see that I'm pregnant as if it's written in red ink on my forehead.

"I told you not to eat so much. That was too much sugar to be eating for one meal." Nope, just judgmental as usual.

"Yeah, Mom, I know. I'm just going to go home and take a nap before my nail appointment. I'm not feeling great."

She looks me up and down and I'm praying she doesn't fight me on this.

"Okay. Go home and rest. Don't let the wedding stress get to you. I have everything under control," she says with a slight smile before turning back to the sink to finish the dishes.

Sighing a breath of relief, I make my way out to my car blasting the air as I try to collect my thoughts. Clearly I gave Cayson ideas with my sexting a couple weeks ago. I am shocked he even had the guts to send me a dick picture when he seemed thrown off by my photo last time. The impending wedding must be a turn on for him. Thank God my mom wasn't the one to open that message. I don't know how I would cope with my mother seeing my fiancé's dick.

Opening my text thread with Cayson, I send him a message.

A dick pic?

Three bubbles pop up almost immediately before disappearing.

Chapter 24

Asher

I can't stop my knee from bouncing as I wait for my ride to pick me up from the airport. I feel like a dick for showing up the day of the wedding, but I had to take care of some things before I could make this happen. I swallow the lump in my throat as the nerves take over when I realize there is a chance this may not work. My sister's words keep playing on repeat in my head: *Give it your all before you give up.* I know she's right. As stubborn as she can be, Ari is wiser than I like to give her credit for. She's young, but she's not stupid.

I know that there's a chance this may go completely wrong, and I may have just torn apart my life in California for no reason. But if there's even the slightest chance that giving up my career will give me the life I want, I *need* with Tate, then I had to take the risk. I still feel guilty when I think about the look on my boss's face when I told him I was quitting. They invested a lot of time and money in me, and I am so glad they never made me sign a contract that would have screwed me out of this chance. I take my phone off of airplane mode and check my email for a response from my advisor replying to my request for a semester off before continuing online next semester. I come up empty, but I'm not surprised considering it's a Saturday.

I considered the options between staying in California for a future career I may not even get versus fighting for a future with the woman I can't stop loving, and she won ten times over, no doubt in my mind. A life without her in it is a life I'd rather not live unless I'm forced to. The car horn honks, and I pull open the back door, throwing in my suitcase before getting in the passenger seat.

"Are you sure you want to do this?"

"I've never been more sure of anything in my life. Take me to her. I need to see my girl."

The smile on Charlie's face reassures me that he thinks this is the right thing, too. While I was completely honest with Tate that weekend in my apartment, there's one thing she doesn't know. It wasn't fate that brought her back to me; it was divine intervention with a little help from her dad. I haven't pressed him about the reason why because I get the feeling that between Cayson and me, I win favorite.

When his text came through telling me when she'd be home, I didn't question it. It was pure coincidence that Tate was coming home to visit the same weekend as my sister's engagement party, and it was pure coincidence that my sister ran into her that morning and extended an invitation. I couldn't understand why I was going home even as I boarded my flight. I kept telling myself it was to see my sister, but I knew I was lying to myself. I wanted closure. I wanted to make her hurt like she'd hurt me. It wasn't long after I laid eyes on her that I knew I couldn't let her go. A quick call to her dad ensured that she wasn't getting home, though the unexpected snow made that much easier to achieve, and while I felt bad asking him to give up his time with her, he was a willing participant in my scheme, and still is as he drives me to crash her wedding.

Pulling into the venue, Charlie points to the bridal suite and exits the car to make sure Cayson isn't going to be a problem. At least not until after I've said what I need to say.

"Good luck, man," he tells me. "I hope she sees what I've always seen. You two are good together. She hasn't been the same since she lost the piece of her that you claimed. Cayden isn't right for her. She doesn't radiate happiness like she did with you. Go get her." He winks before heading in the opposite direction to the groom's room.

I know I'm probably the biggest dick on earth for showing up the morning of a wedding to profess my love to the bride and beg her to have a future with me instead of the groom. But as I knock on the door and it opens to the most beautiful woman sitting in a white silk robe with a mimosa in hand, beaming that smile I love so much, I don't care how much of a dick I am. All I care about is the fact that I'm not the man in that groom suite getting ready to marry her.

"Asher? What–" Tate's gaze meets mine in the mirror before she turns around, jaw on the floor.

"What the hell are *you* doing here?" Mia snaps.

Dismissing her, I walk up to Tate, caressing her cheek in my palm. I sigh a breath of relief when she melts into my touch instead of pulling away.

She looks up at me, tears threatening to fall as she asks, "Asher, what are you doing? You can't be here."

The panic look that takes over her face has my stomach churning as I struggle to say the words I've been rehearsing in my head for hours.

"I just needed to see you. I have so much I want to say to you. I'm sorry I couldn't get to you sooner. I had to take care of some things first, but I'm here and I need you to listen to me, okay? Just let me say everything I need to say before you answer."

She opens her mouth to speak but decides against it as she slowly drops back in her chair putting her glass on the table.

"Absolutely not," shrieks Mia. "This is not happening. You need to leave. Now."

My head whips around to the woman whose presence is not at all wanted right now. I have to bite my tongue as I swallow the urge to tell her to fuck off and leave me alone with Tate. I have to play my cards carefully if I want this to work, and cussing out her mom probably isn't the best way to do it.

"It's okay, Mom. You can take a walk. I'll handle this," Tate says as she clears her throat clearly trying to contain the emotions she's feeling.

"No. I'm not leaving," she spits. "He is."

I bite my tongue as I drop to my knees taking Tate's hands in mine.

"Please, just listen baby. If after you hear everything I have to say, you want me to leave, I will leave no questions asked, and I won't try to contact you ever again. But please, please just let me say what I need to."

Her gaze drops to where my thumb is rubbing her hand before she looks at me with misty eyes and nods slightly. I can see in the mirror as her mom crosses her arms and readies herself to kick me out. The look I shoot her in the mirror has her second guessing herself as she huffs and sits down. Good choice.

I place a kiss on Tate's palm as I take a deep breath and let it all go.

"I won't lie that I was so angry with you for leaving me after graduation. I was angry that you could throw away everything we were like it was nothing. Relationship aside, our friendship was enough to stay and fight for. You were my world, and I know I was yours. I know I fucked up by not telling you about the job offer. I was just so thrown off and surprised, and I knew you were stressing with everything going on that I didn't want to throw that wrench in your plans until I knew how to convince you to come with me. Looking back, I realize that it was stupid.

"You aren't the only one at fault for us ending the way we did. I could have fought harder for you. I *should* have fought harder for you. And I have never been able to stop thinking about the future we could have had if I would've handled that situation differently."

There are tears rolling down her face now as she tries to keep her focus on me.

"You are the only woman I have ever imagined a future with. Seeing you again after so long only reminded me how much I need you in my life. I am so fucking thankful that something brought you home that weekend because those hours with you in my apartment are hours that I will remember until the day I die even if you tell me to leave and never come back. I fucking love you, Tate. I don't want to live a life that doesn't have you in it."

I can see Mia in the mirror scolding me from the couch but I continue.

"You want a big white wedding? It's done. Just let me be the man that's standing at the altar when you walk down the aisle. You want four kids and a white picket fence? That sounds fucking perfect, as long as I'm the man who gets to watch your belly grow with my babies and see you be the amazing mother I know you would be. You want to stay here in Florida? Fuck it, I'll be a Florida man. I'll go fucking anywhere with you."

She's sobbing uncontrollably now, and I don't miss the mumbling curses that Mia is releasing behind my back.

"I will forever regret not fighting for you eight years ago. But even more I know I would never forgive myself if I didn't fight for the future I want with you. Baby, I know you felt it too. I meant it when I said it wasn't just sex, Tate. It was so much more than that. It was a rekindling of the fire that we both lost the day we fell apart. We found it again in that apartment. You are my fucking life, Tate. You. So please, Tate, if there is any part of you that is willing to fight for me, for us, don't walk down that aisle today. Let me be the man who gets to love you until the day I die. But if you truly feel that your future only exists without me in it, I will walk away. But I hope more than fucking anything that you choose me."

"But what about California? You're going to finish law school and be an attorney at the firm. I–" She's trying to talk between her sobbing breaths. "I can't–"

I take her tear stained face in my hands.

"I quit," I tell her. "After you left, I realized I couldn't continue a life in a place that you didn't exist, a place I wasn't happy. I knew I had to give every ounce of fight I had to get you back. You can thank my sister for that."

I wink at her as I wipe her tears with the pad of my thumb.

"I meant what I said, baby. You have my heart in your hands. It's your choice whether you keep it or throw it away."

"You have got to be fucking kidding me."

Tate and I both turn to Mia.

"Are you seriously considering throwing your life away for him?" she shrieks. "Giving up everything you've built for a guy who was terrible for you? Cayson is everything, and I mean *everything* good that this guy isn't." She gestures to me and I can practically see her morphing into the snake that she is as the venom laced words leave her mouth.

"Cayson is perfect for you," she says. "He's got a stable job, he's offered you everything you need to have a successful life with him. He treats you so well, probably better than you deserve sometimes. He wants the same things that you do, and he's serious about giving you the life that you want. God knows he's much more attractive than–" again she gestures to me, "*this* is."

I don't miss the fact that she just admitted she finds Cayson attractive. Every bone in my body is fighting the urge to throw something at this woman and kick her out of the room.

"Be serious, Tate. You can't throw all of this away to get back with him. Clearly you were having more fun in Michigan than you let on. I won't tell Cayson that you cheated on him while he was here worrying about you and planning your wedding. But you better walk down that aisle to him today. You'd be stupid not to. He is perfect for you."

I can't stop the anxiety that starts churning in my gut as I watch Tate and wait for her to respond. Her mom isn't wrong. I'm sure Cayson is the better option. But I'll be damned if I don't try my best to convince her otherwise.

"No, Mom," Tate says. "He's perfect for *you*."

My eyebrows shoot up at Tate's words.

"What the hell is that supposed to mean?" Mia is clutching her chest as if she was just fucking stabbed.

Tate stands, gathering her composure before straightening and staring at her mother. "Cayson is perfect for me in *your* head because he's exactly what you always had planned for me in your head. You've had my life planned out since the minute you left me and Jace in Michigan. You wanted me to go to college, get the perfect job, marry the perfect man, and have the perfect future. Except you never cared about what I wanted. You wanted to live vicariously through me to get the life that you fucked up. That's why you hated Asher because he wasn't what you envisioned in *your* head. I'm sorry your marriage didn't work out, but you don't get to dictate my life anymore. I'm going to live for me and what *I* want, and if I decide to marry Cayson, or not marry Cayson, then it will be my choice, not yours."

Fire burns in her mom's eyes as I see a response brewing in her brain.

"If you loved Asher so much then why didn't you tell him about the baby?"

Her shouted words linger in the air as everything goes silent. I look to Tate and see guilt fill her eyes as fresh tears spill over her cheeks before turning back to her mom.

"How did you know?" she manages through her tears.

"How did I know? Because I was there in that hospital room as you clutched your stomach and cried when the doctor told you that you were losing the baby. I was there, not him!"

I feel like I'm going to pass out as the words filter into my brain, connecting all the dots. She was pregnant when she left, with a baby that she lost. Tears start to fill my eyes as I try to make sense of it all.

"Wait a minute," Mia says. "I was the only one who knew about the miscarriage. You knew I knew about it. So why would you be asking how I knew? Unless… Are you–"

Her mom's eyes dart between me and Tate who's now sobbing in her chair. Her mom storms across the room snatching the mimosa Tate had been drinking from the table and takes a drink.

"This is pure orange juice. There's no alcohol in this is there, Tatum?" Mia asks, accusation clear in her tone.

I turn to Tate looking for an answer as my ears start ringing. I can't gain my composure as I watch her head shake to confirm her mother's suspicion.

"I can't believe you, Tatum. You're pregnant with his baby aren't you? I'm guessing it's safe to say Cayson doesn't know."

Again Tate's head shakes as her body is racked with sobs.

"Seriously, Tatum, I can't believe you were willing to throw it all away for *him*. How could you let this happen? Cayson has done nothing but be good to you and here you are being a... a *slut* behind his back."

Tate runs to the bathroom, and I can hear her getting sick as the toilet lid clinks open. I'm surprised I haven't bitten my tongue off with how hard I'm biting it. I knew her mom was a bitch, but the hatred in her words has me steaming. Her mom turns to me, evil in her eyes as she crosses her arms across her chest.

"Congratulations are in order I guess," scoffs Mia. "Well, maybe. Clearly she's in love with you considering she was about to walk down the aisle to someone who isn't you, and wasn't going to tell you about the baby. Again."

I don't have the will to respond.

"If I were you, I'd leave before you can ruin anything that can't be repaired. She's better off without you, and so is that baby. I'll figure out how to fix this. I gladly let her leave you; I'm not letting her leave Cayson. He's better than you'll ever be, and I'll be damned if I let her, or you screw this up for me."

She gives me one last hateful glare before storming to the door. "Now get the hell out," she calls, the door slamming behind her.

VIII

New Message

To   thirstwithclarissa@gmail.com

My husband's an ass

Dear Clarissa,

I'm three months pregnant. Recently my sex drive has been much higher than normal. My husband has been a big fan of this. However, the other day he told me that he won't have sex with me when I get bigger because it's going to gross him out. I have no desire to have sex with him anymore and he says I'm blowing it out of proportion by denying him sex. Do you think I'm being dramatic?

 Send

Chapter 25
Tatum

I hear the door slam even through the ringing in my ears as I hurl one last time. I strained to hear what was said after I ran to the bathroom but I couldn't stop wrenching long enough to hear anything. I know I'm going to be facing the wrath of my mother but I can't make myself care. I don't know the person she has become the past few years. The woman I spent summer breaks with, the woman I called Mom would have never looked me in the eyes and called me a slut.

Granted, she's not wrong. Cayson has always been good to me, and I slept with someone else, and managed to get pregnant. That truth burns more than the acid still sitting in the back of my throat. I grab some toilet paper and wipe my mouth before rinsing with water and look in the mirror. I look nothing like a bride is supposed to on her wedding day. My cheeks are stained with tears, my mascara has bled, and my eyes are blood shot. I think I popped a blood vessel with how hard I just puked. I knew this was all going to bite me in the ass, but I was hoping I had some more time to deal with it.

I plop down on the floor as Asher's words flood through my brain. He came for me. After the way I left him before graduation, I never deserved any love from him. But with how I left him heartbroken in his car weeks ago, and the fact that I was about to let myself walk down the aisle to a man I don't love, I know I truly don't deserve Asher's heart now. The thought kills me as fresh tears brim in my eyes because he was willing to give me everything I ever thought I wanted if it meant a future with me.

215

The man who never wanted to get married or have kids was willing to give me those things because of how much he loves me.

Oh my god. The realization dawns on me. He quit. Right? I'm racking my brain trying to replay the entire conversation to make sure I heard him correctly. He did. He fucking left everything he has spent years building just to have the chance of getting my heart. Here I was willing to let him go because I couldn't give up the shitty life I've built here that doesn't even make me happy.

As I try to gain my composure, I know that no matter what happens after I leave this room, I can't marry Cayson. There are a lot of things that I have done wrong in my life, but marrying a man that offers me nothing except security is not going to be one of them. I don't know how to fix this, or if I even can, but I owe Asher an explanation. That's the least he deserves after everything I've done to him.

The fear hits me that he's probably already in his car driving away from me, from the possibility of us. I wipe the tears from my face and lunge for the door, throwing it open as I prepare to bypass my mother and her questions waiting for me. Except when I walk out of the bathroom on wobbly legs, it's not my mother who's waiting for me on the couch. Asher is staring at me with red-rimmed eyes, exhaustion, and pain etched on his face.

My breath catches in my throat as I struggle to come up with the words I was ready to throw at him if I managed to catch him before he left. Seeing the hurt I have caused has taken away any sense of logic I had. He rubs his eyes and runs his hands over his face before taking a deep breath and letting his eyes lock on mine.

"I'm so sorry," I manage through a choked sob. "I know you probably don't want to hear anything I have to say, but I owe you an explanation. I owe you so much more than that, but please just let me explain."

I sniffle and he puts his hand out gesturing for me to start talking. I collapse on the chair across from him and let the words flow from my mouth without looking at him because I know if I see the pain in his eyes again, I won't be able to say what I need to.

"I found out I was pregnant the day I found out about the job offer in California. I showed up at your house to tell you about the baby and your mom spilled the beans about you moving. I got so angry because you were keeping such a big secret from me. And then once we started arguing, I realized that I couldn't tell you about the baby. I couldn't let you give up such a good opportunity to stay back and be a father when I knew it wasn't something you had ever wanted. I didn't want you to resent me for making you play a role you didn't want. I couldn't survive having you hate our child, or me for holding you back. So I said what I had to in order to hurt you so you wouldn't want to make it work. I packed my bags and left for Florida right after graduation so that I wouldn't risk you finding out about the pregnancy before you left."

I wipe the tears collecting in my eyes and take a deep breath as I relive the worst time of my life.

"I had a miscarriage a few weeks later. That's the only reason my mom knew because she was with me when I started bleeding. I knew in my heart that I had lost the baby before we even made it to the hospital. A piece of me died that day, and I think part of that is because it was the last piece I had of you. She was furious with me and told me I should never tell you about it because she convinced me you were better off without me, that we were terrible for each other. I didn't know how to heal after it happened, and it felt like everything in my life was falling apart. I had lost you, and then lost the only piece of you, of us, I had left. I knew I wasn't ready to be a mom, but I loved that baby, and I had already begun to envision my life as a mother before I lost them."

I take a few deep breaths trying to compose myself, hoping he doesn't speak up before I get the chance to finish. I chance a quick glance and I see tears in his eyes before I return my gaze to the floor wishing I hadn't looked at him.

"I was struggling with finding a reason to live anymore so I took a semester before starting school. That only fueled my mom's anger more. I wasn't living up to her expectations. Nothing was the same with her after the miscarriage. She started trying to control every aspect of my life and morph it into the life she's always envisioned for me, or I guess for herself. When I met Cayson, she fell in love with him instantly. I think she loved him before I did to be honest. She took every chance she had to tell me how good he was for me.

"Even after he proposed, I couldn't stop thinking about the life, the love I had with you. I thought about you constantly and wished things had happened differently, that I had reacted differently. Cayson is the total opposite of you. Everything was so perfect with him. Too perfect honestly, and it was boring. I knew in the back of my mind that I felt guilty for staying with him when I was thinking about another man. But I let myself believe that we were better off without each other, and Cayson was the right decision. He was the exact vision of what my mom wanted for me."

He clears his throat, and I allow my eyes to meet his before I continue. I want him to see the truth in my words.

"I always avoided going back home to visit Dad because I was so scared that one day I'd run into you, and I knew I wouldn't survive the hurt it would cause to see you, the regret it would dig up. And then I saw you at that party and my heart shattered. I knew you were angry with me for how I left things, and I had to tell myself that you were better off hating me. So I pushed you away from the start. My desire was a mirror image of what I was saying to you. I couldn't stop imagining myself with you, what it would feel like to be with you again. And then we, *I,* let it happen. I let us fall into our old feelings, and you were right. It was so much more than sex. I felt what you did. I felt my love for you burning all over again." I sniffle as I hold back a sob.

"But then the guilt took over. You admitted how you felt in your car, and all I wanted to do was go back to your apartment and spend the rest of my days with you in that bed, soaking in your love. I wanted to throw myself at you and tell you how much I still loved you. But I couldn't get myself to tell you about the miscarriage and risk you taking it all back. And I couldn't have a future with you knowing I was keeping such a big secret from you. I knew you deserved to know, and believe me, all I wanted when it happened was to call you and have you by my side as I grieved my loss, our loss. But I couldn't."

The truth is spilling from me effortlessly because I have owed him these words, and finally airing the truth is taking weight off my shoulders even though I know there's a chance they are falling on empty ears. Ears of a man who has been hurt by my hand too many times to care about my excuses. I let myself continue, hoping that he's listening to every word.

"You have built such an amazing life for yourself out in California, and when I found out I was pregnant this time, I got scared. I was worried I'd have to live through the pain of losing this baby, and I can't survive that again. I was going to tell you, I promise I was. But I told myself I just needed to follow through with this wedding first. I know it's stupid and careless, and I'm such a selfish bitch for it, but I didn't think you'd want to be with me after the hell I put you through. I didn't want to live through this alone. The words you told me ten minutes ago are everything that I have ever wanted. I love you recklessly. I want a future with you. I want to grow a family with you and wake up every morning trying to prove to you that you are more than enough for me, and trying to prove that I will do whatever I can to show you how much you mean to me. I don't expect you to still feel the same for me now that you know the truth, but I at least owed you an explanation. I won't blame you for walking out that door and leaving me without looking back. And I don't expect you to take on this baby if you don't want to."

The relief rolls off my shoulders as I stare at him. I don't know where any of this is going to go, but I feel a sense of freedom now that I've told him what happened. Even if he walks away without looking back, he knows the truth. I fiddle with my fingers in my lap as I wait for him to respond.

"You don't have to say anything," I add. "I know that was a lot to dump on you. Most people would've already walked out that door by now. I can leave if you need some time."

He stands, running a hand through his hair as he blows out a breath before turning to me.

"How could you, Tate? How fucking could you?"

I refuse to look at him as I let the guilt eat at me knowing I deserve it.

"I know. I'm sorry. I'm so so sorry," I say as fresh tears fall to my lap.

"No you don't fucking know."

But then he's on his knees in front of me taking my hands in his.

"Look at me."

I force my eyes to his and see fresh tears forming before one falls down his cheek.

"How could you think for even a second that I would have chosen that stupid job over our baby? How could you go through that grief without calling me and letting me be there while you healed? How could you think with any fiber of your being that I would walk out on my, on *our* child? That I wouldn't want a part of that? You didn't give me a chance."

He sniffles before placing his hand on my stomach and smiling slightly.

"I am fucking pissed at you, but neither of us were in the right. I am so angry that you walked out of my room without telling me you were pregnant, but I'm more angry that you let yourself go through that pain and that grief without letting me be there for you. I still mean every word I came here to say. I still love you beyond words. I still want to be the one that you walk down the aisle to. I still want to be the one who gets to watch you become the amazing mother that I know you will be.

"I can't guarantee that this pregnancy will go the way we want it to, but if you let me, baby, I will be with you every single step of the way. I never envisioned a family in my future unless it was with you. I would've been content only ever having you in my world, but don't think for a second that I don't want the chance to be a father"–that word causes him to choke back tears as he struggles to continue– "to the child that we created. I still want all of it with you Tate, but you have to give me the chance to prove it. I'm not saying any of this is going to be easy, but I don't care about easy if it means I get you."

I can't help the sob that's racking my body as I let his words sink in. As I let in the reality of what's happening knowing I don't deserve any of it.

"You still love me after everything I've done to you?" I ask him. "You gave up your life for me. I'm not worth that."

He takes my face in his hands wiping my tears away with the pads of his thumbs.

"I didn't give up my life, Tate. That job meant nothing to me. It was something to fill an empty void, to make me feel like I was living up to the potential you always said you saw in me. You are my life. You and this baby are my life, and you are worth *everything*."

My tears keep falling, and I can't seem to stop them.

"These fucking hormones won't let me stop crying."

He laughs and presses his lips to mine.

"Mmmm orange juice and bile."

I bite back a smile as I wipe the tears from my face. Even in moments like these, he brings light to the darkness.

"Exactly. That's the best breakfast a guy could ask for," I tease.

"I can think of something I'd much rather have for breakfast."

He winks at me before slipping his hand up my leg.

"What do you say baby? Want to ditch this place?" he asks, and I see nothing but pure love in his eyes.

"I need to take care of some things first. I guess I need to go call off my wedding and deal with my mother."

The thought of telling my mother I'm calling off the wedding is horrifying. I'll deal with her after I talk to Cayson.

"Do you want me to go with you?"

"Would you? I'm not afraid of Cayson, but my mother is a different story."

"Of course. The sooner this happens, the sooner I get you to myself. Let's go."

"Let me brush my teeth first."

I can't help but cringe at the fact that he kissed me after I puked and snotted all over myself. And yet he's still looking at me like I'm the most beautiful thing he's ever seen.

After I've brushed my teeth and changed into a pair of sweats and t-shirt, Asher is eagerly waiting for me and my heart flutters. Pressing myself to him, he lifts my chin and presses his lips to mine. His fingers trail up my sides under my shirt before caressing my breast. A moan leaves my mouth as his tongue plunges in demanding entrance, devouring me, claiming me. Sliding his palm through my hair to cup the back of my head, he dips as he trails desperate kisses down my neck.

"Asher, please."

I'm greeted with a knowing grin as he drops to his knees pulling my sweats to the ground and ripping my panties down with them. His eyes rake over my body adoringly before locking on mine.

"Tell me what you want, baby."

My need for him is so strong that I don't care anyone could walk in here and see what's happening. All I care about is feeling him.

"I want you," I say, fisting his hair between my fingers. I try pushing his head closer, but he resists, pulling back with a devious grin.

"You gotta be more specific than that, baby," he says tauntingly.

"Fuck. Please Asher, make me come."

"With pleasure," he says before diving in and devouring me with his tongue. He moans his approval as he laps at my throbbing clit before thrusting two fingers in my pussy. I've missed this man beyond measure, and as he looks up at me, consuming me, I know that he will always worship me. His fingers pump in and out as he sucks on my clit causing me to scream out. I almost lose my balance as I stumble back, but his hands grip my hips so hard I know I'll have bruises in the morning. The thought of him marking me again only inches me closer to release as he reaches up under my shirt, pinching my nipple between his fingers.

"Tell me you're mine," he demands.

I'm too focused on my need to come that I don't reply. He withdraws his fingers, making me whimper as he pulls away.

"I'm yours. I'm completely and entirely yours," I declare.

"Damn straight you are," he replies before thrusting his fingers in again, swirling his tongue over my clit, adding more pressure as I press his head in closer. He pulls back just enough to blow his warm breath over my aching clit before going back in and devouring me like I am his last breath, the only thing keeping him alive. He adds a third finger and I'm thrown over the edge, climaxing as he laps up every drop.

Pulling back, I grin as he wipes away my wetness from his chin.

"Now *that* was a good fucking breakfast." I chuckle as I pull his mouth to mine, tasting myself on his lips.

"I love you," I say as I stare into his eyes before grabbing my sweats and slipping them back on.

"I love you, too, baby. Let's get this shit taken care of so I can get you out of those fucking sweats again. Plan to be sore tomorrow because once I get you naked, you're mine until you can't fucking move," he says as he playfully smacks my ass and ushers me out of the door towards the groom's suite.

My heart pounds as I try to figure out what I'm going to tell Cayson. Telling my fiancé that I'm pregnant with another man's baby, and that I'm leaving him for said man on my wedding day isn't something I imagined I'd have to do in my life. But as I look down at my hand in Asher's and think about the life growing inside me, I can't wait to get this conversation over with so I can start over with the family I'm meant to have.

This feels right. Picturing my future with Asher makes me feel seventeen again as butterflies go wild in my stomach. The thought makes me happier than any visions of a future with Cayson ever did. I don't want to hurt him because he doesn't deserve to be hurt, but I know there's no way to have this conversation without causing some pain.

As we make our way to the groom's suite, Asher stops me, capturing my lips with his. "If you want to leave at any point, just say the word. I can handle this if you don't want to."

"I need to do this," I say. "I owe it to him. I just may let you handle the conversation with my mother though."

A snort slips free from him at the thought of having to speak to that woman.

"Anything for you baby." He places another kiss on my lips before pulling away.

"Are you ready?" This moment has me thankful that we decided not to have groomsmen or bridesmaids in our wedding so I won't have to deal with an audience. But as I go to reach for the doorknob, my stomach sinks as I hear breathy moans coming from the other side of the door. I turn to Asher and can tell by the look on his face that he hears it too.

"Oh, Cayson. Fuck yes. Don't stop, I'm gonna come."

I freeze with my hand on the knob before Asher takes charge, grabbing it from me to swing open the door. My jaw drops to the fucking floor as I take in what I'm seeing. She's riding him, Cayson's clothes strewn on the floor, his fist in her hair, lips on her breast. They both freeze as the door flies open, slamming against the wall. Her familiar eyes meet mine, expression unreadable as Cayson's eyes widen in horror.

I can't believe it as it leaves my mouth.

"Mom?"

IX

◆

New Message

To   thirstwithclarissa@gmail.com

Advice

Dear Clarissa,
My husband told me he wanted me to try squirting. I tried but I couldn't do it. I didn't want to disappoint him so I peed during sex. He thought I squirted and told me it was a huge turn on for him. Do I come clean or should I keep peeing the bed?

 Send

Epilogue
Tatum

❖

Seven months later

My mind races as I watch a droplet of water slide down my glass. The condensation has me starting to wonder if she's going to actually show. It's twenty minutes later than the meeting time we agreed to. A foot violently kicks my ribcage, and I rub my growing belly, smiling when he pushes against my hand in response. Every day becomes more uncomfortable as my baby continues to grow, insistent on making room even when I'm convinced my body has none left to offer. I know I'll miss feeling his kicks once he's born so I'm letting myself love the pain as he shoves his foot right into my bladder.

"Sorry I'm late," she says. "There was a wreck on the highway and I forgot my cell at the hotel. I get it's a small town, but you'd think they could build a hotel within twenty minutes of this place."

It's been six months since I've seen my mom. Walking in on her fucking my fiancé wasn't exactly healthy for our relationship so I left them both at the venue not waiting for an explanation. I left that day deciding to live my life for me. Not settling, not worrying about my timeline, just living to be happy. Part of that involved moving back to Michigan to be close to Jace and my dad.

Mom and I have been on the outs since my wedding day. When she reached out last week asking to come meet me, I didn't know how to feel, and staring at her now, I still don't. But I will admit that seeing her again after six months has my heart aching because she's my mom, and I miss her. I stand up to hug her, removing myself from the booth which looks anything but gracious I'm sure as I try to maneuver my pregnant belly around the table. Her eyes instantly fill with tears when I make my way to her.

"Oh my gosh." She goes to place her hands on my stomach before pulling them back, clearly afraid I won't allow it. I grab her hand placing it on my belly, watching her face light up when he kicks her hand.

"Look at you," she says. "You're glowing, Tate."

I return her smile as she wipes away her tears and sits down ordering a tea when the waiter approaches. I'm at a loss of words so I let her take the reins, not knowing where this conversation is going to go. When she realizes I'm not going to speak up first, she lets herself talk.

"I'm sure you're wondering why I asked to meet you," she says. "I know you didn't ask for one, but I owe you an explanation. I never meant for you to find out about Cayson and I that way. I guess if I'm being honest, I wasn't planning on you finding out at all."

I admire the fact that she's being honest.

"Although I'm surprised you didn't connect the dots after you saw the picture on my phone."

"What picture?"

She pauses as if she's contemplating telling me if I haven't already figured it out.

"You know, the day before the wedding. You checked my phone and saw the picture of his–"

She looks around the restaurant before putting her hand up beside her face to cover her mouth from anyone else's view.

"His penis," she whispers.

"Oh my God! That was meant for you? I thought he meant it for me and accidentally sent it to the wrong person."

It all makes so much more sense now. I wondered why he seemed so nonchalant about it when I brought it up later that night. It wasn't something I expected from him, but apparently his spicy side comes out for my mother. I bite back my smart ass reply that it's bigger in pictures than real life. Although I guess she already knows that. Ew.

Her cheeks flush with embarrassment.

"He told me you texted him about it and I realized what had happened. I thought about cutting things off with him so many times, but I just couldn't."

She takes a sip of her tea tracing her finger through a drop of water on the table.

"It wasn't something I planned," she continues. "After Cayson proposed, I could tell you weren't as invested as he was. I was angry for him because he was so good to you, and I could tell he was trying so hard to make you happy, but it was never enough."

Looking back now, I know she's right. Cayson and I never would have worked because I was trying to convince myself that I was happy with him because our relationship was what I thought I had to be happy with. It was conventional.

"I am so sorry for treating you the way I did," my mom tells me. "I blamed myself for leaving you kids. I wasn't the mother I should have been, and I did everything wrong. I wanted so much more for you, and I know that's no excuse for how I handled things. I was trying so hard to get you to live your life better than I lived mine, but I only hurt you and pushed you away in the process."

She pulls her eyes from mine, taking a drink of her tea, pain etched on her face.

"Don't ask me why, but I felt compelled to come here last night into town after I checked in to the hotel. I guess I wanted to reminisce on what things were like in this small town. I'm not saying I did it the right way but I am glad I got out of here. This was never meant to be home for me."

She throws her hands over her face muffling her words.

"Shit. No. That's not what I mean."

She looks up at me clearly hurting at the fact that she can't figure out how to say what she means, and then she goes on: "You know I loved you kids; you two are my world. God, I just can't get this right."

I see the hurt etched in her features as she pulls back into herself across from me thinking she's screwing it all up again. I reach across the table taking her hand in mine urging her to look at me.

"I know what you mean, Mom. You weren't a bad mother. I won't deny that bouncing back and forth between you and dad was tough, but it's okay. I know we've had our struggles, but you're allowed to be happy."

She closes her eyes and takes a deep breath as if she's trying to gather her thoughts before speaking.

"I just mean that looking back, I know now that my home was always going to be somewhere else in the end."

I know she means Cayson, and the look in her eyes tells me she's waiting to see my reaction. Looking at her now, the irony dawns on me that she's been struggling with the same battle as me. Fighting the battle of doing what you think you're supposed to versus doing what you want for you and no one else.

"I only wanted you to be happy, Tate. I was just so convinced that I knew what was best for you even if you didn't. I could tell how much

Asher meant to you when he showed up in that bridal suite because the way he looked at you is the same way Cayson looks at me."

Her last words tell me that her and Cayson are still together and it doesn't bother me like I thought it would. I knew it was a possibility; I just had to wait for her confirmation.

She reaches across the table taking my hand in hers.

"I need you to know that I love you so much, and I will never forgive myself for hurting you the way I did. But I also need you to know that I love Cayson. I know it seems wrong for so many reasons, but we found something in each other, and by the look of that ring on your finger I have a feeling you know what that feels like. I know you do because you felt it a long time ago in this same town."

There is no cruel intent in her words. She's seeking *my* approval which feels strange after seeking hers for so long.

"Cayson deserves to be loved by someone who loves him wholly," I say. "If that's you, if you find solace in each other, then I'm happy for you as long as you're happy."

A lone tear slips down her cheek as she smiles the first genuine smile I've seen on her face for a long time.

"Just don't expect me to be calling him my step daddy when you two decide to tie the knot."

She laughs, stifling her cry and I know that we made it. I have my mom back. For better or for worse with how it happened, I got her back.

"I am very happy," she says a tear falls down her cheek landing on the table. " I'm not asking you to forgive me right away, and I know it's going to take some time, but you're about to be a mom. I want to be able to witness that. I want my daughter back, and I want to be able to meet my–" She gestures to my stomach.

"It's a boy."

"A boy. I'm going to have a grandson." Another tear falls down her face, and it dawns on me how screwed up we let things get.

"I'm not saying it will be easy to see you and Cayson together. I'm going to need an adjustment period."

"Understandable," she laughs slightly, relief clear in her voice.

"You are my mom, and I miss you. I want my son to know you. But I also need you to know that I am happy too. Asher is everything I need. He balances me. He is my heart, my solace, my missing piece."

I place my hand on top of my belly. "This right here is everything I could have asked for in life. I had convinced myself for so long that I needed to live my life a certain way to please you, to live the way the world has taught me I'm supposed to, when all I needed to do was do what made me happy, and this is it. If Cayson is your happiness, then I'm happy for you."

She nods her head with misty eyes and in this moment I know we will be okay.

✛

Two hours later, many tears have been shed and we both have a better understanding of each other. She tried to call it off with Cayson the day I walked in on them together, but he refused to let her walk away. Hearing about their relationship while strange, was also heartwarming because I know in my gut that he is happier with her. I explained to her that Asher and I are not getting married. He got me the ring as a gesture, but we both felt content leaving the legal paperwork out of the equation.

The baby is due soon, and mom will fly back to be with me after he's born. The thought of being a mother scares the shit out of me, and I needed her to be there when it happens. It's going to take some time for her and Asher to hash out their relationship, but I have faith they'll come around to each other.

Mom and I walk out to the curb where Dad is waiting to take me home. He's gotten rather protective while Asher is busy and refuses to let me drive by myself since the baby could be here any day.

"So when I was walking around last night, I went into the community building," Mom says. "Those photographs are amazing, sweetheart. Though I do have to say, I have a favorite."

She places her hand on my belly again and I grin because I know which one she's talking about because it's my favorite, too. In the community building, Asher's photographs line the far wall for everyone to admire. It brings my heart so much joy knowing people finally get to see in him what I always have. Right in the middle of the wall is his piece of work titled *My Heart*. A photograph of me, growing belly standing by Admiral Finley in the park where our story truly began. Flowers freshly blooming for spring in pastel colors around me.

I give mom an awkward hug laughing as my baby bump puts a large gap between us. Dad walks around to help me into the passenger seat.

"New truck?" Mom asks.

"It is," he says. "It was time to move on to something new."

I wave mom goodbye as we pull away, finally feeling completely at home.

Asher

◦◆◦

Fourteen months later

"Babe, we're gonna be late!" Tate yells as she chases after our son who's giggling as he trots his way over to me, arms outstretched.

"Dada, up," Weston says as he smiles up at me.

Bending down, I hoist him up onto my shoulders and he instantly shoves his tiny fingers into my hair trying to steer me around the house in the direction he wants me to go. Tate stares at me, irritation clear on her face as she worries about being late for our flight. I bend over holding onto Weston's legs and place a kiss to the top of her head.

"It's fine, sweetheart. We will have plenty of time."

My reassurance clearly does nothing as she rolls her eyes at me and continues to scramble around the house shoving last minute things into her carry on.

"We won't have plenty of time," she says. "By the time we get to my dad's to drop off Weston, you're going to insist you go in to say hi and then you'll end up talking for an hour as if we didn't just see him last week, and we'll be late!"

"Take a breath, honey; it'll all be okay."

I lift Weston off my shoulders and set him on the ground as I grab our suitcases. Tate follows behind holding Weston's little hand in hers as we walk out to the car. I can hear her mumbling behind me that I'm a liar and we will in fact miss our flight. Little Miss Planner still hasn't gotten used to going off of her schedule even with a toddler, and as we found out last week, a baby on the way.

As I pull out of the garage, I pull her hand to rest on my thigh even though she continues to mumble as she stares out the window. Looking in the rear view mirror I can see that Weston is already asleep, his mouth wide open. He's a mouth breather just like his mom.

I pull in the driveway of Charlie's house where he's waiting eagerly with the door open. That man never gets more excited than when he gets to see his grand baby. Tate looks over at me expectantly as she waits for me to get out of the car.

"Take Weston inside," I tell her. "I'll wait out here."

As much as I really would like to go in and chat with Charlie for a while, I don't want to prove her right and listen to her gloat about it the entire drive to the airport.

She hops out of the car and unbuckles Weston, laying his sleeping head on her shoulder as she totes him up the stairs to Charlie who doesn't hesitate to take him from her with a beaming smile on his face. They exchange a few words before he's closing the door and Tate is racing back to the car. Watching her giddy with excitement for our trip makes my heart soar. She's so beautiful, and every day that passes I still wonder how I got so damn lucky to call her mine.

Leaning over the console I push her door open and watch her climb in.

"What are you grinning for?" she asks as she buckles her seatbelt.

"You're just cute."

She scrunches up her nose at me before kissing my cheek.

"You ready to go?" I ask.

"So ready."

I pull out of the driveway and turn up the radio, smiling when Tate starts singing along to the country song that is played at least twelve times a day on this station. She glances over at me smirking when she notices me singing the words, too. I can't help it. She got me hooked on this country shit.

Our trips are always fun, but this one is special, and I smile to myself at the fact that Tate doesn't know I'm surprising her. We travel regularly now that we got our business up and running successfully. It was her idea, a traveling couple's photographer and intimacy counselor. Human Nature was also her idea for the name. Rather fitting, if you ask me. We travel all over the world, getting to see everything I have dreamed of seeing. At each destination we post our services on a travel site where tourists or locals can book with us. She offers intimate counseling to help couples strengthen their bond, or explore their intimacy in the bedroom, while I offer photography sessions whether they be sweet photos on the beach or romantic spicy photos.

The business does surprisingly well and offers us the best of both worlds. After my internship at the magazine failed several years ago, I never expected I'd get to make a living while traveling the globe with the woman I love most in the world. Often times Mia and her husband Cayson travel with us and watch Weston while we're working.

Things were awkward for a while after Tate called off the wedding, but we all surprisingly get along really well now. Weston loves them both, and I honestly couldn't picture a life without them now. It's funny how life has the strangest ways of working itself out.

"It feels weird not having Mom or Cayson with us this time. I can't believe they were too busy to come to New Zealand. I bet it's gorgeous there."

She smiles as her hair blows around her face, her hand stuck out the open window.

"Not as gorgeous as you baby." I grip her thigh and blush creeps across her cheeks.

Little does she know Mia and Cayson are coming on this trip. Her mom is already at the hotel waiting for us. She had to get there a day early to ensure she could get the dress there without Tate finding out. The ring on her finger has been a symbol of our love for each other for the past year. She still says she's completely content with our life as it is and doesn't need a wedding, but I know better. While I wanted the ceremony to be small and intimate, I knew she'd want her mom to be there to witness her daughter get married. I never thought I was the marriage type, but for her I'd do anything to make her happy, and while I know she'd go the rest of her life without an actual marriage, I want to be hers completely.

Bringing her hand up to my lips, I kiss her fingers before placing my hand on her belly. Looking at her now, I know my life is complete. She gave me everything I could have ever wanted, everything I never knew I needed. My heart is full, and she's the reason.

ACKNOWLEDGMENTS

To my husband for encouraging me to turn my love of romance into a book of my own. Thank you for being a listening ear as I vented about my characters, and aired my frustrations when I couldn't gather my thoughts. Thank you for being my support even in my times of self-doubt.

To my editor, Michael, thank you for believing in this book. You saw my vision and pushed me to make it the best that it could be.

To my readers, thank you for taking a chance on this newbie author. Nobody knew I was writing this book besides my husband, and my constant encouragement was knowing that people would get to read the pen I put to paper. The words contained in this book mean the world to me, but they'd mean much less without anybody to read them. I can only hope you fell in love with Tate and Asher as much as I did while writing their story.

About the Author

Emma Humfleet is a romance fanatic who aspires to be like those responsible for writing the books that made her discover her love of reading.

When she doesn't have her nose buried in her Kindle, she's busy chasing her ten-month-old son through the Indiana home she shares with her husband.

Heart in Your Hands is her first novel.

Curious readers can reach Emma via her alter ego at thirstwithclarissa@gmail.com